I0771084

# STATION OF THE BIRDS

## Betsy Sussler

SPUYTEN DUYVIL
NEW YORK CITY

For Dickie Landry and Tina Girouard

## New Orleans

New Orleans shimmies: formed from a swamp into a Creole capital, it's all sweat and longing, the sweet smell of decay and wild, wild wails. Fortunes were amassed on its Cotton Exchange where any crop—sugar, rice, or cotton—was used as a man's collateral; the Exchange no longer exists, but the cries of the slaves who planted and harvested the crops can still be heard. Now it's skyscrapers that rise from the Mississippi mud. A crescent dangling from the southern tip of Louisiana, the city should be underwater, but the levee holds the river back. River full of cargo ships loaded with containers from the Middle East, South America, and the Caribbean. New Orleans's docks line the Mississippi and encroach upon the city's old French Quarter, a cat's paw for transient jangle and intransigent corruption, its indigenous inhabitants—members of secret societies or the offspring of illicit unions—are concealed behind fastened shutters and wrought-iron fences. Lush courtyards camouflage the entrances to hidden apartments.

Uptown, west of the Quarter, in the Garden District, gracious mansions shelter New Orleans' aristocracy. Their homes stand alongside former slave quarters, now shotgun cottages and guesthouses. Daryl Monroe, young scion of the unattainable, a visitor at one of these mansions, wants to inhale it all. And he has been, if one considers "all" to be cocaine. Draped in Salome's seven veils, silk fluttering over well-formed limbs, eyes lined with kohl, Daryl wears no mask; it would get in the way of his tongue and nose. Golden in daylight, hazel at night, his eyes have seen more than he cares to acknowledge. Daryl entertains one wish: to escape into oblivion. His body is a vessel; three or five presences whir inside him and they're having a conversation spanning centuries, raving in tongues. He's privy to their rage—mendicants and prophets haunt his drug-induced frenzies. Through the din he hears a tentative honky-tonk. The piano's out of tune; he knows this for a fact, screaming, "Throw the miscreant off the balcony—that'll tune it up!"

His fellow revelers, former fraternity brothers, oblige him, leaving the startled pianist behind. The Steinway is pushed through open French doors out onto the gallery, but the men are too drunk and laughing too hard to lift it over the railing. Daryl starts a countdown, and one concerted shove sends the piano crashing through the banister. A black shadow in the night, it lands on the front lawn, a symphonic crash. Residents of the Garden District, those in white houses with galleries and balustrades, don't often display anything this dramatic on the outside. Inside's another matter.

Men costumed in togas or black cloaks redecorate the premises to fit their mood. They've lowered sparkling chandeliers to the floor, crystal prisms on Persian rugs illuminate bare legs and feet. It's October in New Orleans and all evenings are hallowed. Dipping moths flutter and burn in the bulbs. The ceiling's garland of plaster cherubs, replicas of beaming infants, chattering and effusive in the light, is ghostly in the dark. One sport, a skeleton painted over a black leotard, pulls down the velvet curtains. Daryl yells, "Toss 'em around the room, like they just flew in."

This is Kappa Alpha, a place to which he no longer belongs, having completed his college sojourn six years ago. The party's not bad in his estimation—just not high enough. Which is why he's come back and what they need him for; his experience in matters of excess constitutes his authority. It's past midnight and the female guests have left or slunk upstairs with their consorts. The men partying with Daryl are the ones who didn't score. He calls to them from the darkened parlor. Daryl's tits are fake, preposterous balloons, but he has what they want. He's a belly dancer, his skirt white tulle, his earrings gold rings. Daryl pops the balloons and his bosom deflates, rubber sticking to little brown vials of glass containing the only snow fully appreciated south of the Mason-Dixon Line. The term has always amused Daryl, calling it "blow" when the real ecstasy is in the inhaling. Eager young men crowd around him. Daryl empties seven vials of cocaine onto the glass-topped bar.

"All manner of gratitude accepted. Just don't kiss me unless your tits are real."

The record player blares Dizzy, but the neighbors can't complain. They're all here, busy getting educated. The library's closed and this is Alexandria before it burned. Daryl's surrounded by the initiated, doling out knowledge in a silver spoon, when someone he calls "The Pedantic

Asshole" flits into the parlor. The man's dressed as Little Lord Fauntleroy, the only one in a mask. To make sure he gets no pleasure from snorting or licking, Daryl has noted this before. His mask is askew. Its pubescent, smiling lips hang below his chin and crop his neck, but a lace collar holds his ensemble together. Fauntleroy acts as if he's innocence personified, but Daryl's well acquainted with desperation masquerading as youth. The idiot is waving a pistol as if it were a magic wand claiming he can make Daryl disappear. Daryl's pretty sure he could, if he were to aim. It's time to cut more lines, everyone's snorted them up, but Daryl's distracted by the gun. All around him, men step away.

Fauntleroy makes a sweeping gesture encompassing the room and its occupants, screaming. "This is my place; you gave it to me!"

"You little ingrate, I set you up." Daryl's incensed. "And what I give is mine to take. You want to take what's mine?"

Lord Fauntleroy doesn't like conundrums; he flaunts his pistol. "You can't come back here; you hear me?" A snide reminder, "I have too much on you."

Daryl saunters up close to Fauntleroy, ignoring the gun, eyes flashing, and snarls. "Listen to me, you son of a bitch. I go anywhere I like, whenever. So lift my veil and kiss my ass." Daryl turns his back on Fauntleroy but he hears the trigger cock.

"Paradise."

Hell, thinks Daryl, it's all the same to me. He turns to see Fauntleroy spinning the pistol chamber.

"You haven't been there."

Daryl could argue this point, but Fauntleroy suddenly screws the gun in his own ear Russian roulette style.

Jesus, not this tired old game. Daryl stalls. "Oh, come on, don't do that."

But Fauntleroy's too busy postulating, "The power of God is within me, I can see Him."

Daryl's thinking that it's not a monotheistic universe; something vast is taking up residence inside him, too.

Fauntleroy pulls the trigger: nothing. A collective sigh, opinion is set—the man's nuts. He hands Daryl the pistol. Daryl is almost certain it's not loaded, but he's not in an obliging mood, pride being his other sin of choice, so he spins the chamber, aims at the ceiling, and BAM, blows a hole into the plaster overhead. A cherub drops onto a chintz couch; dust coats the oriental rug. Behind his rubber mask, Fauntleroy grins. Daryl waits in dead silence as the bedroom contingent mumbles and gropes its way down the stairs. Couples in dishabille, laughing and swearing, step around glittering chandeliers and into the parlor. When his audience is assembled, Daryl empties the chamber and hands Fauntleroy the gun.

"Take it easy, asshole. I'm not spoilin' your little setup."

But Fauntleroy, if nothing else, is a showman. He pops another bullet in the chamber, starting his dare all over again, spinning the chamber, aiming straight at his temple this time, gloating. "I told you He's on my side. I can see Him."

Fraternal opinion remains firm. Someone yells, "Don't be a fool!" The room's breathless. Daryl tries to stare him down, but Fauntleroy presses the barrel to his temple and doesn't flinch as he fires.

Daryl flinches, wondering if the man has just seen God. Fauntleroy has fallen where he stood, limbs splayed. Blood oozes from his wound, from his ear, pours from his mouth. A woman starts screaming. Daryl kneels and presses his fingers against the man's neck searching for a pulse; the skin is warm. Fraternity brothers gather around them; someone murmurs, "Jesus." The mask has slipped from his face, its grin now lopsided and grotesque. Daryl removes it altogether. The dead man is blond and impish, his face prematurely lined. A quiet hysteria is taking hold. Escorted women wrapped in improvised shawls make furtive exits to escape scandal. Those positioned around the corpse break away, leaving Daryl alone to guard the body. Men huddle, speak in whispers. A preppy in a ponytail, who considers himself Daryl's friend, comes to his side: "It would be better for us if you were to go, so we can call the cops."

Easy for him to say, it's not his fingerprints all over the gun. Daryl yells over their heads. "Sweep this place, I want it cleaned in five minutes. I'll call the damned cops."

They say that if you make your money by illegal means you must live simply and hide your wealth. Daryl has always ignored this maxim, claiming instead that his wealth was inherited. And if he were to admit that he had to earn a living, Daryl would point out that drug dealing's no different than selling real estate except that it's more visionary. There had been a time, not long gone, when he was a fixture in New Orleans society. His privileged friends had accepted him because he was one of them; and back then, when his lifestyle was sanctioned, he flaunted his money, graciously and generously. His original clientele attended the university with him. The privileged inherit the earth by insisting upon their privilege. No one Daryl knows in New Orleans is meek. And none of them discuss their prerogatives or, as time passed and his dealing became more overt, Daryl's role in their lives. But they wouldn't mind discussing his minor role in this man's death—not with the local police—but spitefully, among themselves.

Do not misunderstand. Daryl was born into wealth, and he assumed that that advantage would always be available to him. But he was denied his inheritance. It hadn't been lost, but rather, it had been lost to him. A few guessed his secret, more and more as time went on—there was no home to return to, no money with which to purchase a future. He had lit upon the quick and ready cash that comes from drug dealing to cover his subterfuge and keep his pride. Daryl mocked privilege by mimicking its presumptions; the common law did not apply to him. Initiating the uninitiated, hanging with the wild boys, none of this was new; it suited him. There was a snobbery attached to drugs, an in-crowd mentality that Daryl mined well. Hard work and scholarship never occurred to him, although he worked hard to maintain his rich-boy image. And while rumor could only hint at his predicament, everyone was aware of his dealing.

After graduation, Daryl's friends moved on to the business of social standing. He did not fit into this equation. His contemporaries who remained his customers became more covert in their arrangements with him, and he was left to the younger men who could afford that sort of indiscretion. What came next was Daryl's new reputation—not that of the wild scion of an old Southern family, but one defined by the slump of failure: a rudderless albeit spirited man who had become addicted to his excesses.

It takes Daryl no time at all to come to the obvious conclusion: absence, like death, is a negation. It will lessen further damage. There can be no pleasure in talking about him behind his back if no one can see the effect of it all on his face. And while Fauntleroy's death hastens Daryl's flight, he has already felt the winds of exclusion. There is no place left for him in New Orleans. There were a few who had seen his core: no angel to be sure but not confined by the lurid gossip that informed his reputation, he longed for more than the self-obsession that absorbed him.

Daryl stayed in town long enough for the death to be declared accidental. Packing was quick, he had few possessions, and his apartment, rented by the week, had come furnished. Everyone Daryl knew he'd already had in one form or another, and vice versa, there was nothing much left to say. No ties had been his rule for some time. What he owned was replaceable. It would seem a sorry state of affairs, to leave the place you've lived with no friends left behind, but that's precisely what Daryl wanted. Mercurial by nature, dogged by design, these are the attributes he carried with him.

## -2-
## THE ATCHAFALAYA

One hundred miles west of New Orleans lies a swamp of neck-deep water, scrub pine, and oak. Cottonwood, bald cypress, and ash spring from bayous choked with hyacinth. The world below the waters, as the world above, lies suspended, murky with tree trunks, dense with moisture. Herons, at dawn gray, at dusk deep blue like the hyacinth, dive through the vines and rise, squirming fish caught in their beaks. This is the Atchafalaya, water pocked with land, where all substance roots in sediment and thrives in heat. A wanton maze of muddy bayous and ambling creeks contorting into the Gulf of Mexico, Louisiana's great waterway to the Caribbean and buoyant host to the offshore oil rigs along its coast. Concealed coves and shrouded islands have offered sanctuary to smugglers since Jean Lafitte and his pirates helped Andrew Jackson's Louisiana boys defeat the British at Chalmette Plantation. Locals believe that Lafitte buried his gold in the Atchafalaya, and that to this day herons fly with rare coins in their beaks. Outsiders are not privy to this information. Louisiana has a history of complicity; the unspoken is sustenance.

At the tip of the sweet water, just before a brackish marsh meets the Gulf, Michael Duvet meanders south in a battered aluminum skiff with a black Lab sleeping in its bow. Michael is riding on the other side of midnight, his sight thwarted by a new moon, when his boat knocks against a trunk. A shade in the dark, Michael slows his motor to listen. His dog wakes, sniffing. Sound travels clear and crisp over the marsh: it's another motor. The dog whines. A speedboat takes shape from the dark, banging the skiff in its wake. It contains three men; one is holding an automatic rifle and another steers. Their boat slows down long enough for the third man to toss Michael a knapsack. Then they're gone, their motor purring into the distance.

A wading bird spreads its wings and dawn breaks. Michael guides his skiff through a tributary bordered by black willows into the beige waters of Bayou Teche. In early morning light, Michael appears to be all-American but a little too world-weary for his twenty-seven years. He is wearing camouflage gear, as if he were a hunter; an adequate disguise in the rural south, where even the white oligarchy is partial to killing its food. As the sun rises above the riverbank, Michael squints: a blonde girl-child with flowing hair and a long white dress leads a kid goat to the shore. Sunlight diffuses in the humidity; the girl waves at him, her hand a pendulum, as he guides the skiff into a tangled cove.

The shoreline is bordered by a neglected pecan grove: its trees are heavy with nuts, their limbs sagging, and the overgrown pasture is scattered with husks. Another black dog, part Lab, part hound, runs howling into the water, jumping and clawing at the skiff's bow. "Hey Beauty, hey girl, yeah, we're home."

Past the grove, the Duvet farmhouse looks abandoned, raised on cement blocks against the floods. It used to be a general store, plain and square, its back porch tacked on like an afterthought. Michael's home needs a paint job, white chips flake from its clapboard like snow. He hunkers down and crabwalks under the house into its crawl space. The smell of mildew permeates a loamy storage dump of oars, beach chairs, and an old mattress for the dogs' bed. His Lab crawls after him on its belly, panting and sniffing. Michael buries his knapsack behind the mattress; he's too preoccupied to sense twigs snapping and husks being mashed into the grasses.

Beau Duvet comes strolling up out of the grove, picking nuts off the ground, cracking their shells, tasting their meat; a latent sexuality charges his gestures. Muscular and compact, but he's past his prime. Beau looks around the farm as if he's carried the smell of the place with him. His resemblance to Michael shocks strangers, that and his difference: thirty years older with features aged by hard living.

The dogs smell Beau's scent and bark. Michael remains hidden and silent in the crawl space.

Beau calls, "Bubba, Beauty. Come here." Bubba wriggles out to jump on him. "Where's your master, huh? Where'd he disappear to, out carousing all night?"

Michael holds his breath, watches the animals prance on hind legs and wag their tails, listens as they lumber after

Beau up the speckled steps. "Finally get himself a piece of ass?" The rickety door slams shut.

When Michael enters some ten minutes later, he feigns surprise, "Beau!" Their home smells makeshift: a morning damp seeps through the floorboards. The wood-burning stove stands cold, ceiling fans rotate in the draft. Beau and the dogs are sprawled over an old couch covered with camouflage tarps.

Beau's had his moment; posters plastering the walls attest to this—"Beau Duvet, Live in Chicago," "Recorded on the Bayou," "The Saint Martin Playboys,"—and also record his disintegration, a progressively aging Beau, once front and center, now hovering in the background. In most of the posters, he's the only white man with various Black musicians.

Michael's gaze drifts over a heap of battered amps and speakers, and Beau's guitar case. "Didn't know you were comin' back so soon."

Beau shifts. "Statewide tour: Baton Rouge, Lake Charles, Port Arthur, points beyond—canceled."

"Sorry to hear that." Michael escapes to the bathroom.

Beau shouts after him. "Where've you been?"

Michael yells. "Took one of those damned hunting parties out."

Blocking the doorway to the bathroom, Beau asks, "Who?"

Michael's washing his hands; they're clean but he soaps

them up again. "No one you'd know."

"Where's your gear?"

Michael looks around for a towel and finding not a one, shakes his hands dry. "You stickin' around awhile?"

Beau's moved on to the back porch.

Michael follows him, shoving the screen door open, letting it bang behind him.

Beau's lying in wait: "What about the grove? Pecans need harvesting."

"Can't find labor."

Silence as each one sizes up the other.

"Hey, sit on down here, talk to me."

Michael stalls. "That's my chair."

Beau spreads his burly thighs over the cane thatch and leans back. "This chair? The one I'm sittin' in? I ain't movin'." His gaze leaves Michael to follow a black line of cypress along the horizon: dark birds circle a pale white sun. Beau turns back to his son. "You partying with me tonight? Welcome me home?"

Michael sits beside him. "Yeah, sure, long as it's Richard's, 'cause that's where I'm goin'."

A causeway crosses the Atchafalaya swamp basin. Pilings support a cement road that refracts the monotonous thumps of a car's tires onto a metal guardrail. A two-lane highway spans ninety miles of dark still waters; it's a lonely empty stretch where a car could speed and crash, or glide, flying over the guardrail to sink into the soft fragrance of rotten fauna—the carcasses of drowned deer, wounded muskrats, and broken-winged ibises—that lie submerged under the water. The dead fertilize the swamp's flora, its cypresses, willows, and islands of wild cane.

Daryl Monroe drives his insect-shaped Corvette over the water; its headlights sweep the trees that line the causeway. The trunks are hypnotic in the headlights' glow, their images duplicate before him as he speeds past those that were once ahead of him. Daryl has to shift his vision back and forth from darkness to the silver-gray trunks in order to stay awake. His only change of scene comes suddenly; illuminated by his headlights, a mist in the shape of a gyre floats through the trees and fades away. Daryl scans the swamp beyond his windshield, expecting the shape to reappear. A dull gray fog rises instead, enveloping his car in an eerie cocoon, vanquishing the trees, and reflecting the car's headlights back into his eyes. Daryl follows the studs that support the guardrail on his periphery, steering his car along its path.

As a child, he would watch the mist form at dawn as it wandered over the waters and disappeared into the forest. He'd lie back in his boat, pretending to fish and observe great blue herons gliding after it on gusts of wind. In the swamp, birds would dip and swoop as if borne by Gregorian chants. Of this Daryl was certain: the birds could hear refractions, the sound of chants traveling through time, Liturgical cycles repeating. A whisper could shoot past Venus, echo off Saturn, ricochet around a demon star back to the birds, who were, he used to imagine, the winged confidants of spirits.

Daryl Monroe would like to forget, but he can't. It takes much less time for him to return to his hometown than he spent thinking about it all the years he's been gone. St. Martinville lies in a corner of the Atchafalaya swamp on the shores of Bayou Teche. Sugar, crawfish farming, and trapping muskrats comprise its legal industries. Daryl intends to establish himself in its illegal one, smuggling. Protected by Louisiana's maze of bayous, it's a livelihood dating from the time of Lafitte's pirates, enduring through prohibition, and with the new drugs, in Daryl's estimation, ripe for development. All he has to do is find one link to the trade; that would be enough for him to locate its source. Conveniently enough, that one link, if rumor holds any truth, is the boy, now a man, with whom Daryl spent most of his youth.

-3-
## ST. MARTIN PARISH

Daryl's childhood home sits squarely in the center of St. Martin Parish, on a working sugar plantation surrounded by cane fields. It had been his mother's place, and her mother's before her, in their family for over two hundred years; ever since successful slave revolts in Haiti, what was then known as Saint-Domingue, made the cultivation of sugar in Louisiana suddenly seem preferable, at least to the French colonists. Cane was still grown in Saint-Domingue, but the revolution precipitated a transfer of ownership from the white population to the Black population. The colonists fled to Louisiana, where it's Black people even now who work the fields. Green shoots darkened by night, stalks piled in heaps; everything else forsaken for the harvest. Daryl drives down the access road as if he owns the place, surveying the crop. Carts and tractors litter the rows, cane fields cut to stubble spread out past the mill. The mill's machinery is manned twenty-four hours, two shifts a day, to get the cane harvested before the rains begin—dense, gushing rains that start with little warning and then stop just as quickly. Fieldworkers are lighting fires in the ditches and the bagasse bursts into flame, illuminating the sky. Embers spit at a tenuous night. Daryl stops the car; the smell of burnt molasses is so thick he wants to lick the air. The mill's lit up like a birthday cake; smoke from its chimneys belches up to the stars. The field hands and mill workers have done plenty: roots have been replanted in the sand and mountains of raw sugar are piled in the mill's sheds. Daryl turns from the fields, the work at hand, and drives up an oak-lined avenue toward the main dwelling.

He walks into the plantation house via the old slaves' entry and looks through glass panes at what used to be his mother's land; behind him, the parlor is still and dark. All that he allows himself to think is, Nothing's changed, same old antique shit hasn't even been moved. He wanders through her seating arrangements as if he's a ghost and tries to enter the library, but its French doors are locked. Cupping his hands around his face, Daryl presses his nose to one of the panes and peers into the room, winged waterfowl— his father's prized taxidermy collection—are scattered over antique tables. He contemplates breaking a pane and unlocking the door, but sighs instead, turning away. A half-circle of chairs placed around the piano as if for a concert beckon to him. Daryl pauses at the keyboard and tries a few phrases from Chopin. "Jesus," he mutters; it's out of tune.

Scents rise as he opens the sideboard, jasmine and tea rose cling to linen. Searching between the crisp, cool sheets Daryl slips out a black-and-white photograph of his mother. The silver frame is curved and tangled; she's younger than he remembers her. Even in the dark he sees her smile, her hair gray, but in life it was ginger red, falling past her neck. He wants to hold her. Her eyes—hazel like his—embrace him in a glance. This is only his mind playing tricks. But her arm is flung over a young boy's shoulder, and the child's face is eager with happiness. Daryl can't remember ever being loved like this. The glass between them is soft and cold. When Joseph Monroe comes down the stairs with his rifle, Daryl's too absorbed to notice. And when Joseph sees that it is in fact his son, he says, "So it's you, Daryl. Lucky, I didn't blow your head off."

Daryl looks at himself in the photograph, a young child laughing, his mother's arm his sanctuary, and answers, "This can't be me."

He leaves the way he came, headlights searching, swerving his red Corvette around the plantation's driveway like a threat. The way to Michael and Beau's seems easy after the causeway, a two-lane blacktop that runs from Louisiana's Gulf coast to the Texas border. Daryl speeds past dirt-poor farms, their fields planted with sweet potato and soybean, the land flat and vast below a black horizon.

The Duvet house still looks as he remembers it: hippie heaven. It smells like mildew and roach spray. No one is home, but two black dogs are sleeping on the couch, gnawing flea-bitten flanks even as they dream. They wake enough to growl but can't be bothered to bark. Must have had a long day, Daryl concludes, as he surveys his old hangout, Beau's image forever present in the posters that hang everywhere. Once upon a time, Daryl sought Beau out as an idol, the only local white musician brave and crazy enough to openly cross the color line and brag about it, just in case anyone missed his act. The Federal government's attempts to desegregate Southern Louisiana had only partially succeeded. Each parish comprises a country unto itself in which the races rarely mix except under proscribed circumstances, all unequal and inequitable. Throughout St. Martin Parish, this arrangement has always included covert sexual unions. Anyone could see it. Subsequent generations of the African population turned shades of brown, yellow, red, and gold. Hence the one-sixteenth laws, no longer legal but readily applied as the accepted way. If you lived in Louisiana, having one great-great-grandmother of African descent and every other forbear of white descent, added up to you being Black, and your prospects there dimmed accordingly. Birth certificates were altered to escape the rule; families were destroyed by racial pride or shame, alignments and lies. Hostilities and loves, filtered as they had been through successive generations of lighter-skinned mixed-bloods, created hierarchies within the Black community that were as controlled as those beyond its periphery. When Black people prospered, they kept to their own enclaves to avoid white scrutiny.

Yet through all the prancing, shuffling, and snobbery inherent to any caste system, Beau Duvet did as he pleased. He crossed over, mixing and playing with whomever, whenever, answering only to himself and what he loved: music. Black musicians admired him, white musicians tolerated him, but none denied his talent. Whether Beau's bravura stemmed from courage or some perverse refusal to conform, Daryl isn't sure, nor does he care. There's one other place he wants Beau and Michael to be. Turning from Beau's posters, the unkempt room, his once familiar refuge, he heads for it.

Zydeco is washboard strut and accordion bawl, the raunchiest, wildest sounds to come out of the sweet water, providing you understand Cajun French, in this case Black Cajun French. Lyrics translate into "Baby won't you fuck me tonight?" The patois might be archaic, but the sentiment's timeless. Richard's dance hall used to warehouse sweet potatoes. A long wooden bunker burrowed into the earth; one bare bulb over a weathered door indicates the club's entrance. The best way to find Richard's is to arrive late; then the field outside its blackened windows doubles as a parking lot, and secondhand cars and battered trucks hugging both sides of the road indicate the spot. Daryl parks under a streetlight, then saunters toward the twang of electric guitar and an accordion's moan.

"Hey, man!" A teenager calls to Daryl from a spanking new sports coupe. He hangs out his window, proffering a joint. "Hey! Got ID we can use to get inside?"

Daryl peers into the car. "Don't carry ID."

The teenagers are white and wearing clothes that mimic their parents' country club attire. A coiffed woman-child in the passenger seat beckons. "Why ever not? You got something to hide?"

"Yeah, I'm too old to need it."

Inside, past the single white bulb and a door so low

Daryl has to duck, a pasty white sheriff collects the entrance fee. He stops himself from laughing, a holster hoists up the sheriff's stomach so everyone can see his pistol. A purple light illuminates the cash box, revealing the date just stamped onto Daryl's hand: 10.28.1981. Its glow reveals a harvest of dead flies littering the floor. Richard's is strung with electrical cords dangling twenty-five-watt bulbs; the turquoise paint cracked all over the plank walls reminds Daryl of a latrine. Saturday and just past midnight, the club is packed with Black workers drinking and dancing. At the other end of the warehouse, past high-stepping couples, Beau's on a stage of raised plywood, strumming his electric guitar with Clayton Fontenet's band. "I sing like a girl. I sing like a frog. I'm a lonely boy, I ain't got no home."

Daryl wants to sink into anonymity. Dark eyes glance at him with distrust bordering on scorn. Whites enacted the one-sixteenth laws to defend the bloodlines against their own marauding. Ask any white man within fifty miles. He'll support his colored mistress and their offspring until the children get old enough to ask too many questions, and then he sets them loose. The children have no idea where they belong, but the old law does.

The warehouse is soggy with heat and Daryl's thirsty. Liquor can't be bought at Richard's; the patrons carry it in in brown bags. Mixers and beer can be purchased, but they're out back. Daryl works his way through the crowd. He too is wearing his country club clothes, pastel pink pants and a wintergreen golf shirt, so when a huge man in an orange

Zoot suit slaps his palm, he knows it's appreciated. Beyond the dance floor, Daryl spots a girl working the shadows; she sees him and a current of attraction flashes between them. This is not what he's come here for, but she's exchanging something in the palm of her hand for some cash with the Zoot. The Zoot looks high enough, but Daryl never judges another man's habit. He checks to see what the white trash with the pistol is doing: the sheriff's staring right at the girl, watching the whole thing go down. Daryl spends most of Beau's set observing her and the cop, wondering if the sheriff owns her, or who it is that's paying him off.

By the time Daryl saunters out back, men are pissing in the bushes more often than they are drinking. A couple of acres of weeds and flatland, a picnic table passing for a set-up bar, and there he is: Daryl's old friend, Michael Duvet, a beer in one hand, a joint in the other, alone. "You're late," he says.

By about ten years, Daryl thinks, but decides to let it slide. "And you?"

Michael shrugs. "Same old shit."

Regardless of Michael's stasis, things have changed. Michael and Daryl spent their early school days glued to each other's side. At Catholic school, which suited neither boy; the Christian Brothers despaired of ever channeling their intelligence. On weekends, Daryl escaped the questionable riches of his own home for the Duvet farm, both boys sprawled in the same bed, under a feather quilt during the damp winters and mosquito nets in the long summers. Michael's grandparents had raised him; country folk, they offered a simple bounty. But the real draw was Michael's father, Beau. He came and went as he pleased. That he was a musician who sometimes earned a living at it, on the road most of the time, was the source of his greatest charm to both boys. Beau romanticized the hard hours, two-bit dives, and sporadic pay into stories of adventure worthy of adulation; but his freewheeling, nomadic life took its toll, and as the boys grew into adolescence, they heard in Beau's stories and saw in his person more and more despair.

It was a demoralizing fall for the three of them, Beau's once gleaming presence marred by circumstance. As they cleared adolescence, the boys' love for him turned to ridicule, and the threadbare poverty of the Duvet household began to embarrass Daryl. He used leaving for university as his excuse to end their friendship. At first, they would meet during holidays, but that soon stopped. Michael felt demeaned by Daryl's opportunities, and Daryl resented what he saw as Michael's false pride, his provincial swagger. He had loved Michael, and he had loved Beau even more, but he left them both behind, his best friend and their fallen hero, because he thought there would be something more to his life, something better awaiting him.

Michael hunkers down against a part of the wall Daryl hopes hasn't been pissed on. His shoulders are clenched in defense; a can of beer blocks his face.

Daryl starts to apologize, "I've missed all this..." and stops before he says he's missed Michael, too; it would sound like bullshit.

Michael sneers. "Heard about you living it up in New Orleans. Don't remember you invitin' me down to visit."

"Yeah, well . . ."

"Yeah well, you must be real busy."

"Not really." Daryl smiles; small talk never held much interest for him either. If Michael doesn't want to get reacquainted, he can cut to the quick. "You also hear I have an alias?"

"That's why you come back here, where everybody knows your family, to change your name?"

Daryl's testing, "For business, yeah."

Michael frowns. "Then you better keep your name; 'round here people only do business with those they know. I need a chaser, you want one?"

Typical, Daryl thinks; first he doesn't want to play, then he does. He follows Michael and almost smacks right into his wet dream, her face like an Abyssinian cat's: golden eyes, golden skin, black natty hair barely held back with a string of leather he can't wait to set loose.

Michael's being polite. "Daryl Monroe, Monique Bouchet. Monique, Daryl."

Men only want other men's women. If she's not Michael's, Daryl can stop wanting her.

# 4

# THE DEAL

Clayton Fontenet was on his last song; he'd already left the stage two times over to cheers for more, when they cleared out to avoid getting caught in the soon-to-be traffic jam parked outside. Daryl sniffed around for the sheriff, but he was nowhere in sight. Beau too, was gone. When Daryl gets to his Corvette, he tosses Michael the keys, and gets into the passenger seat, figuring he'd give him a thrill. It worked. Michael is in heaven, driving so fast, he's throwing Monique off the gearbox and into Daryl's arms. Daryl doesn't mind. Neither does Monique, but Daryl can see Michael eyeing them. As he remembers it, the only emotion Michael lets anyone see is anger, so Daryl figures, what the hell and offers Monique his lap. As soon as she's sitting on his thighs, Michael shifts into neutral, slides the car off the road, and says, "You ride the way you used to, she can have her own seat."

They say Faulkner used to ride standing on the hood of his car, arms spread like Winged Victory over Mississippi roads, blacktop, dirt, it didn't matter. Some friend of his driving, someone he presumably trusted. Daryl performed this stunt as a teenager to impress the girls, wind holding him vertical, silhouetting his frame; the friend he trusted, Michael, at the wheel, peering out the windshield at the road beyond Daryl's braced legs. Faulkner claimed it helped his writing. Faulkner didn't need any help writing, except a bottle now and then. And Daryl didn't need much help with the girls. What he loved was the rush, balanced above spinning tires, speeding over the asphalt, and his triumphant arrival at a levee party or a roadside bar. Daryl's still pretty good at it, albeit out of practice, his arms stretched, hands grasping air.

In Louisiana, in the eighth decade of the twentieth century A.D., you can go out into the middle of nowhere, to arrive at the end of some obscure bayou nobody travels, a piece of marsh along the coast where only the muskrats swim, or some abandoned village, and find an outpost: a helicopter pad for offshore riggers or a platform for pumping natural gas from the swamp into the mainline. Flames rise from fields all over Southern Louisiana, like graves for unknown soldiers. They burn from valves that release the gas expanding in storage tanks buried under those fields; the release keeps the tanks from exploding. Michael turns off the road toward one of the flames, bumping over tractor ruts until Daryl's had enough of his balancing act and yells, "I'm going to throw up."

Michael stops the car.

They're sprawled around the flame as if it were a campfire, the Corvette lurking by the road. Monique is leaning up against Daryl's thigh as if daring Michael. Moths hover around the flame, occasionally bursting into embers. Michael's obstinate; they banter about how he makes money ten different ways while Daryl's gotten nowhere. The silence is stodgy and heavy between them, but Daryl's persistent. "I hear, Duvet, you have the stuff that made Coleridge spit out *Kubla Khan*."

"It's a private club, Daryl, you can't just join; you got to be invited. You ought to understand that."

"So invite me."

"No one's selling you anything."

"I'm not asking you to sell it to me. I'm askin' you to give it to me."

Michael laughs, "What for, past ten years of absolutely nothing?" That's the kind of joke he likes, Daryl thinks, the ones that aren't funny but poignant. But Daryl can tell he's hooked, because then Michael asks, "What is it you have to offer?"

Daryl stares at Monique.

"She knows everything, say anything you want, front of her," Michael says.

Daryl strokes her face. "That true? You a sphinx?"

Monique smiles.

Either way, she's smart enough to keep her mouth shut. Daryl says, "I know there's a drug line coming up the bayous through the oil platforms and I want in on it. You give me what I want, and I'll give you all the cash up front. Once we unload it, we split fifty-fifty."

Michael stares at the flame as if he hasn't heard. Anyone could see his objection, and he's right: the deal's too generous, too quick, and too tempting.

"And if you don't do it, somebody else will." Or, more

to the point, what Daryl doesn't say: And put you out of business.

"Providing I have these connections."

"Providing you do." Daryl stands, looking down at Michael. "Your daddy has; reckon you do, too."

Michael follows Daryl's lead back to the car, hissing after him. "Where do you get the nerve after all this time? Breeze in from any old where, say anything you want, and get what you want."

"Not anywhere. Here. With all these people so familiar with my family name." Daryl holds out his hand for the keys. "I'm driving."

Daryl drops Monique off first, at Michael's insistence, grinning a mock farewell at her lingering one. Michael walks her to the door, but chivalry won't help him now that Daryl knows where she lives. Her cabin is situated on a dirt road off the highway, in an enclave of identical cabins scattered in a clearing. A heavy rain begins to fall, and all Daryl can see of Monique's cottage from his car is the screened-in porch, lit by a hurricane lamp, and then their silhouettes as she brushes past Michael and into the house. They drive back to Michael's Ford Bronco in silence, Michael lost in thought, Daryl smiling in recognition; some things don't change. The dancehall is dark when they get there, rain pounding its tin roof. Michael gets out of the car with an "I'm beat, see you around." Daryl decides he's pushed hard enough. There's time.

A deluge of rain like a waterfall floods the land; puddles the size of small ponds spread across the country road. Daryl drives with the Corvette's top down, retracing the route back to Monique's. He drives too fast, shivering from the rain and the cold, his car crashing through water. Fields on either side of the highway are littered with trailers set back behind crops of stunted crops; mobile homes dwarfed by the land. Rain soaks the Corvette's leather seats, washing away mud from the tires, dead insects from the windshield, and everything Daryl's ever felt. He needs extremes. The wind blows the clouds west; the rain passes as quickly as it came. The moon is full.

It lights Monique's face. A cow-horn crescent hangs above her bed. Incense sends a lazy curl of smoke up to a crucifix, Christ dangling, his legs lifted as if they'd cut off his balls. Monique sleeps with one arm tossed like a child's, palm up, her fingers grazing her cheek. Nostrils flare. Daryl enters the room, throwing the door open so she'll wake. He's breathing hard from the cold and the rain, and he's soaked through, his clothes sticking to his skin. Monique starts, stark naked under the sheet, full breasts, round belly, and rises, tight-lipped, livid, and sways right up to him—Daryl thinking, Proud cunt, neat little curls—in order to slap him hard across the face. They both lose their breath.

She speaks in a whisper. "It's not that easy."

Daryl smiles. "It's not that hard, yet."

"You want me, you court me."

"I'll court you, gladly, but why wait?"

Monique stands her ground, about two inches from his. "I don't like one-night stands."

Truth is slippery, but Daryl wouldn't mind a longer haul. "Depends, doesn't it?"

"On?"

He looks into her eyes and sighs: On how long it will take to set up his business. "I'll stick around as long as you want. How long you want me to stay?"

He doesn't like how vulnerable that makes him sound, especially as she doesn't answer, just thinks about it. But he knows when a woman's about to break so he turns away from her, a slow but determined stroll toward the door. He wants to hear her plead.

"Daryl!"

She's quick, this girl. He likes that: "Dance with me, *cherie*, dance."

Monique runs into his arms and before he can close his eyes, she's wrapped her legs around his waist. Before long, he's deep inside her, skin like velvet. They're on fire, his tongue salt. And she's calling his name. Daryl forgets what he's really come here for. The rain's back again dissolving the earth, pounding the tin roof, and they're humping against the bedroom wall, gasping and crying. The storm passes again, and it's quiet except for their cries and Monique's still calling his name, but Daryl withers and comes unglued, screaming like a banshee. Monique is calling for God.

The stalk of incense has become a dull ember. Daryl's stalling time, entwined in her sheets making pillow talk, Monique's hair tickling his chest, when he remembers.

"What's your relationship to Michael?" he asks.

"He's my brother."

Now this is news. "That a reference to civil rights or something?"

"My half-brother."

"So, which is it, you half white or Michael half Black?" Daryl's joking; they don't make them paler than Michael, but she's serious.

"My mama asked me to deliver a letter to Beau Duvet, Erath, Louisiana."

Daryl does a quick calculation: If the mother looks anything like Monique, and she has to, because Monique certainly doesn't look like Beau, she's some gorgeous colored girl. Beau humps her for a few weeks; he gets another gig, he's gone. Years later Monique shows up on his doorstep with the letter. Out loud Daryl says, "Wish I could've been there."

"Beau was away, Michael answered the door."

Lucky for her, Daryl muses, Michael's gullible. Beau would have run, guilty or not. He wonders if Michael still needs Beau the way he used to.

"They never had a whole lot going, my mama and Beau." She looks at him head on: "It was a fling."

"Where is she?" he asks.

"She died."

"I'm sorry." He hugs her. "I'm sorry." She doesn't cry, just lies there quietly.

"I used to look at every white man I'd see wondering if it was him."

"Well, don't look at me."

This makes her laugh. "He didn't marry Michael's mama, either. She left Beau, pinned a note on Michael's diaper, *Your idea, you take care of him.* Never came back.  Beau's folks raised Michael, left him the farm after they died."

"Monique, Michael and I grew up together."

She takes this in, a stranger to her own brother. "Michael takes care of me."

"Yeah? How does he take care of you, Monique? You work with him or for him?"

That's it; she's out of Daryl's arms, straight and haughty.

He softens it for her. "I saw you passing it, along with everybody else, like the cop at the door."

# 5

# The Will

Waking in Monique's arms takes Daryl by surprise. His usual routine after sex was to lie awake until the woman's breathing softened, listening for any signs of restlessness, and then gather his clothes and slip out into the dawn.

This time, he's curled into Monique like a baby as she disentangles herself to start biscuits and grits. Daryl stays in her bed, content to stretch and scratch. The crucifix gives him pause; he instinctively crosses his legs in defense. Monique comes back in and crawls on top of him, aligning her body with his, brushing his groin with her pelvis. Daryl could have her again, but he has other plans. They dress, bolt down breakfast, and head toward the plantation before the morning is gone.

In the rural Catholic parishes of Louisiana, agrarian rites—those found in the New Testament and others brought to the colony by African slaves—are practiced during the spring planting and again at harvest time: cyclical prayers for bountiful crops and their return. Daryl has situated his Corvette by the access road to the plantation's cane fields, Monique at his side, fixated on the spectacle before them. Empty carts await the harvest as black-robed priests swish smoking censers around a bishop waving a golden miter with outstretched arms. They're traversing a stubbled field strewn with fallen cane bundled and damp from the rain.

A multitude of Black field hands and mill workers follow them. Laymen and clergy swarm the field, reciting the bishop's prayer. A humming sound like bees, the Latin incantation, rises through the heat. The bishop chants a tale of resurrection. "What you sow does not come to life until it dies. And what you sow is not the body that is to be."

Daryl snorts in disdain. The sight of so many clerics, hated masters of his early schooling, calls up his own associations: farting hypocrites—disturbing the vermin, rats nipping their toes, black skirts riding up around their ankles, snakes crawling round their testicles—how the hell would they know? Daryl starts a proprietary accounting: state law sets the limit, six rat hairs for every thousand pounds of raw sugar, after that, seven, eight rat hairs, sugar won't pass inspection. Believe that one, Daryl snorts again, and you'll believe anything—far too many archaic laws in Louisiana, as far as he's concerned.

Daryl's gaze sweeps the crowd. His father is nowhere in sight; priests spook him as well, and their supplications for a donation to the church are rarely answered. But those in overalls and those in khakis, their livelihoods dependent upon each successive crop of cane, have crossed their hands in prayer. Hasn't done a whole lot of good, Daryl thinks, it's already rained; their time is up. They should be getting the cane off the field before it rots, but no, field labor, mill labor, managers, the whole superstitious sorry lot are bleating after the Scriptures, mud caking their boots, sun parboiling their brains.

The blessing is not what Daryl's come here for. He hasn't told Monique anything, but he's planted her by the field like a decoy to see what she will bring to him. Daryl needs associates, and given her background, he's certain that she knows some of the labor. Monique isn't a talker, but he can see her thinking. She has no peace, he knows that much. He leaves her alone. "I'll be right back."

Monique slides herself down the leather seat and plops her sandaled feet up onto its dashboard. Clusters of departing priests, cassocks limp from the damp heat, stride through the muddy field toward the access road. They've finished the rites. The labor turns to the work at hand, gathering the cane before the next rainfall. Daryl crosses paths with a pale-haired acolyte and sends him a fetching smile as he enters the field. There's no place else to go; he has to leave Monique alone if he wants to find out who else she works with. Noland, his father's foreman, sees Daryl coming. He's slouched down so low in his truck that Daryl thinks it's empty until he spots the furtive eyes darting behind the steering wheel.

Daryl saunters up to two Black field hands loading a cart with cane. "That your boss?"

The men keep loading.

Daryl shoves his hands into his pockets. "Guess so." He twists and turns, shifting his line of vision: fields and field labor, that's it. "Sorry son of a bitch, Noland, our age and his life's already over." Daryl's the only one laughing at his version of Noland's dilemma.

The men are too wary to respond, dark irises glazing over so he can't see in.

They've spotted him with Monique and smell trouble.

Well, what are you going to do?  Daryl shrugs. He needs somebody brave anyway, which doesn't stop him from snorting in Monique's direction, annoyed enough to push their discomfort. "See that girl in the car?"

They keep working, thinking, Crazy white fuck.

They're right. Daryl persists. "Pretty ain't she?"

Noland drives up in a cloud of dirt, although he could have just walked over. The field hands push their cart away, leaving Daryl talking to air. "Get no pleasure from your foreman, none at all."

Noland leans out his window, a hometown boy gone to seed, thinning hair the color of dung. "Daryl, anything I can do for you?"

"Not that I know of Noland."

"Your father know you're back?"

"Consider that your business, ask him."

Noland tries another angle in case there's been a reconciliation. "You want, I can open the guest house."

But Daryl's just spotted what he wants; he's talking to Monique, golden colored like her, dressed in khakis and a button-down work shirt. He's no field or mill hand, one better, a supervisor, and he's leaning all over the Corvette as if he could give a damn about Daryl or what's his. Handsome, taller than me, too, Daryl observes.

"Nice of you Noland, but I have a place to stay."

Daryl's almost up to his car when the man takes leave of Monique and looks him straight in the eye, swaggering past him like a dare.

Daryl watches him walk away and asks, "Who's that?" He can smell Monique quiver, taste her excitement. It's the combination, him and the Black man that's enticing to her. Her trembling makes him want her again.

"Someone I used to know." Monique stares at Daryl with something close to hostility.

And why not? Daryl reckons, Black is not white, sex is predatory, and I'm the enemy.

Daryl's father, Joseph Monroe, is too engrossed in his accounts to notice Noland skulking about the library's veranda, waiting for his presence to be acknowledged. Joseph had wooed and married the wealthiest, most beautiful woman available to him, the undisputed queen of sugarcane heiresses. He had earned his degree in Louisiana law, the French code, and after they married, he controlled his wife's wealth. Over the years he found innumerable excuses to take her assets—both of which—her physical attributes and her land—suited his purposes. Since her death, Joseph rarely leaves the library, except to sleep. He's filled it with talismans of her domain—now his—and more. Joseph Monroe needs to own everything he sees: Hundreds of leather-bound books, classics and rare editions, fill the shelves. Maps of the Louisiana coast, the Atchafalaya swamp basin, and the Gulf of Mexico cover the walls. An astrological chart of the heavens hangs from the ceiling. Clocks set for distant time zones are oddly silent. Taxidermy—a possum or two caught in exaggerated crawl stalk the baseboard, but swamp birds predominate. Ibis and egret, all types of herons—black-crowned and yellow-crowned night, great white, great blue, and Louisiana red-necked—crowd the room with glassy-eyed stares, wings trapped in false flight. Logs burn in the fireplace fall, winter, and spring. The telex spews news, but it's encased. Silence reigns. Fresh camellias entombed in glass cloches linger.

Joseph finally looks up to see Noland strolling around the room's periphery, perusing the books as if he were reading their titles.

A sardonic "No-land?" stops him.

"I'm off, sir."

"Why tell me?"

"Thought you might like to know, your son's back."

Joseph doesn't respond, turning his attention back to the numbers.

Noland shifts around, trying to read Joseph's reaction. If you were to ask Daryl, he would say that the man's illiterate in every respect.

"If there's anything you need me to do?"

Joseph doesn't look up. "I'll bear that in mind."

Joseph Monroe was little better than white trash himself, until studying nights, working days, and finally armed with a law degree, he managed to impress the corrupt powers spread throughout the government of Louisiana with his shrewd defense of a racketeer, his erudition, and his capacity for liquor. He also educated himself in the ways of a gentleman—hedonism embossed with a cool decorum. That's how he won over his wife-to-be. She had the same wild streak and the same self-serving respect for the traditional ways as Joseph did.

People thought Joseph didn't care enough about his wife, that he'd married her for her money. He did marry her for her money, but he loved her. Their affection was poisoned by the fact that she came to recognize his avarice and felt used, seduced for her wealth. Fueled by resentment, she took her revenge and seduced in spades anyone she wanted, sporadically leaving both husband and son. Each time she left, Joseph could have professed his love for her to bring her back, but he was too proud, and she must have sensed his need for her, because she always returned. Yet what he wanted even more was a piece of her, and each time she did return he'd take more to compensate for the previous loss, and what he couldn't get from her person he'd take from her land: her sugar cane, her alfalfa fields, her mill, her family's home. Joseph Monroe spread his holdings over the earth and, with the discovery of oil off the coast, under the sea, and when this wasn't enough, he'd simply cling to her. But when she finally happened on a way to leave him for good, Joseph watched over her with a constant tenderness that lasted until she was gone.

Daryl would come back from New Orleans to find her

lying on the couch by the fire, a book slipping from her fingers, her gaze always drawn through the glass panes, past the freshly mowed lawn, pruned branches, and shrubs of her beloved gardens to the birds riding high in the air and the cane fields beyond.

She hadn't made a will, and Daryl hadn't had the heart to ask his mother to do so. She had little left in her name by the time she died in any case. He'd come back for a few days at a time to stroke her palms and read to her out loud. It was hard for his mother to concentrate, but he found that *Metamorphosis* would hold her for a time. Joseph would stand at the door to check her progress, but he never entered the room when Daryl was with her.

She left Daryl nothing in the way of earthly goods. His father took everything, denying his only true competitor for his wife's affection and her coveted lands. He envied his son, encouraged Daryl's dissolution and his private schooling, both of which kept him far from the plantation. That Daryl might legally take back her wealth by claiming his right to inherit in the courts, Joseph has guarded against with payoffs and offshore accounts. His theft is complete, and yet Joseph Monroe still fears his son; he fears retaliation for the harm he has done him, that Daryl might return like for like, malevolence with revenge.

# 6

# ERATH

By noon the mill's furnaces are roaring. Humidity contains the rising smoke, pressing it back to earth. Daryl has tried to find out more about his rival, the man who was leaning all over his car, but Monique will only reveal that he lives on his own and works in the sugar mill. Daryl needs to keep moving whether he has any place to go or not, so they head for the Duvets'. Monique seems content and happy to be with him, and he likes having her around. Her silence, when it's not frustrating his attempts, soothes him.

They arrive at the farmhouse uninvited, tempting hospitality as the black dogs bark from the doorway. Monique lags behind, anxiety holding her back. Daryl doesn't seem to notice, he strides into the house, almost knocking the screen door off its hinges, Monique trailing after him. When its occupants spot her, the action stops short. It's one open space, there's nowhere to hide. Michael does a double take but pretends seeing Monique with Daryl doesn't throw him. He's in what passes for a kitchen, hovering over the oven for Beau's flapjacks, eggs, and grits, wearing a flowered apron. Beau has been wolfing down his food faster than Michael can flip. Beau plays most nights, and by the time he's had the requisite number of drinks he needs to unwind after a set, he can't sleep; a shot of bourbon and a beer chaser sit by his plate even now. Michael makes a show of pecking Monique on the cheek, and Monique gets even quieter. Beau won't look at her, but he's effusive with Daryl. "Sit on down, y'all, Michael bring our guests some coffee."

Guests! The woman's his daughter. It dawns on Daryl as he sits beside Beau that they're insulted that he's brought Monique here, as if it were his prerogative to invite her to their home. Daryl knows Monique better than they do and they're irked because it's clear he's had her, heard her speak in sighs, made her crave. Sons of bitches, Daryl thinks, they should be offering her a place in their home. He sidles a glance her way; Monique's looking at her lap, shamed. Daryl wonders how much time she's actually spent with Beau, reckons it's precious little. Michael slaps a pot of coffee and mugs in front of him and strokes Monique's hair. She looks up at him with such a sadness Daryl's heart cracks.

Beau takes up the slack. "I missed you last night, you son of a bitch. Where've you been? What you been up to? Michael, get these folks some food."

"We already ate, Beau." Now we're folks, guess it's nothing personal. That's fine with Daryl, but Monique's another story. She's got one of the black Labs in her arms, the dog sniffing her face while she strokes its head. He could swear it's smiling. Beau's gone back to being oblivious—that's part of his charm—but it doesn't fool anyone.

Beau passes the cream. "Here, sweetheart."

That's all she wants, Daryl thinks, just a word from him, a small act of kindness. But Michael says, "She drinks hers black," verifying that Beau hardly knows her. No one speaks.

Monique turns her head so they can't see her tears.

Daryl covers for her, "Yeah, been down in New Orleans, living it up, real blast."

Beau's overcompensating, "I played New Orleans, used to play there all the time."

"Anytime you want, Beau, I know all the club people," says Daryl, implying that Beau doesn't anymore.

But Beau's past shame. "Sweetheart, do you know what I used to do?" It's a rhetorical question, but Monique looks up at him as if he were the answer to her prayers. "I'd take this one," indicating Daryl, "out camping with Michael and me, and we'd sing and drink all night. Then come dawn, I'd take 'em hunting." Beau leans back, satisfied.

Monique emits a polite little "Huh."

Beau's smile resembles a snarl. It occurs to Daryl that wolves sing, a cappella. "Surprised to see you're still up to it Beau, an all-nighter that is."

Beau props his leg up on the table, snakeskin cowboy boot an inch from Daryl's nose. "You bet I am boy, last month played three nights and three days hardly a break, stood so long my feet swelled, had to cut my boots off, lost a toe. Want to see?"

Daryl leans back. "Another time, Beau. Thanks anyway. Didn't Michael tell you? I'll be around awhile. We're going into business together."

"Really?" Very sardonic edge.

"Yeah," Daryl calls out over his shoulder, "What the hell is it you do for a living, Michael?"

Michael's retreated, slamming pans into the sink. "I take dumb fucks into the swamp and trap deer so they can shoot 'em, Daryl."

"Well, I'll be damned." Sorry excuse, but it'll do.

Monique lets out a sigh like a tornado.

Daryl takes her cue and says, "We're going boating," excluding Beau. "Came by to see if Michael wanted to take us."

Michael's had enough; he tosses the apron. "Let's go." And he's out the door.

Daryl was aiming for something a bit more graceful.

Beau helps him out. "Y'all come by anytime."

And that's how they leave him, his foot still up on the table so as not to lose face. And if Beau feels abandoned because Michael has chosen to go with Daryl, the boy, now a man, who left them both behind, he's not ready to say it.

Michael has moved his skiff, docking it at Leroy's Landing, which is their first problem. Leroy never bothered to take the whites-only sign off the picnic tables after segregation came under federal scrutiny in 1963. The outdoor eating area, overlooking the muddy Bayou Teche, is full. The house serves hamburgers and hot dogs, period, from a little shack-turned-kitchen on stilts. An unappealing locale, except for the pale skiffs moored off the dock in the river's crook. The waitress discourages tourists by telling them the hamburger's made from alligator. Monique struts by picnic tables seated with entire families chewing overcooked meat.

She smiles down on all of them, munificent in her tolerance of their redneck ways, barely concealing the fact that she's grateful to be in their domain. The adults are speechless, stuff-mouthed and gaping, and their children leer. Daryl dawdles behind to guard her progress, admiring her fortitude. Monique is oblivious to the contempt. He reckons she's inherited that from her father. It's Michael who retraces his steps and maneuvers them all safely to the dock.

Half a mile down the Teche, the vegetation has turned as brown and tired as the river. The sun burns the sky white, islands of wild canebrakes wilt. The only human voices in the swamp are their own, their laughter bouncing over the water. Daryl's draped over the bow, checking out Michael's skiff: it's old, but the motor's new and expensive. The dogs have curled up under the helm to nap in its shade. Michael hears a crackling in the distance and instinctively ducks. During their season, hunters have limited sight through the scrub pine. The boat's cruising straight for a flatbed clogging up the bayou, loaded with dirt bikes and automatic rifles; its occupants are wearing army fatigues.

"Everything a sport could possibly need for whippin' through forests sniping at deer," Daryl jokes. "Hear you coming in a two-mile radius."

Michael's warning, "Armed," causes them both to glance toward Monique.

One of the men has his back to their skiff, tinkering with the motor; the others stare at Monique, they're sneering.

Monique's not afraid; she stares them down. Daryl admires diffidence under any circumstances, but Michael panics and guns the motor. It stalls, the boats drifting side by side, the flatbed rocking with ferality, kissing and sucking noises. The black Labs rise up snarling and instinctively place themselves between Monique and her would-be acquaintances.

Daryl's prone for sunbathing, but he readies himself. "You got nothing to suck, try your ass."

One of the men, spittle sticking in his lip, groans. "Plenty to suck, gi' tha' liddle colored pussy to uhs, boy."

Daryl rises to his full height and screeches, "Soooeey, Soooee," as if calling a pig.

"Daryl, sit down and shut up!" Michael jumps the motor.

But Daryl's busy splashing gasoline from Michael's can over their deck. The dogs back into Monique's legs, whining at the fumes. Michael hears a gun cock, but nobody else is moving except the man tinkering with the motor, he stands up.

It's Noland, his father's foreman. "Take it easy, Daryl."

Too big a coincidence, Daryl thinks, he and Michael both moonlighting as hunting guides. Gives them both license to wander the bayous anytime they please without suspicion. Daryl puts a cigarette in his mouth and asks Noland for a light. Noland's so nervous he nods like he means to give it to him. Michael rips the motor, and they're off, accelerating so fast they disrupt a flock of ibis feeding by the shore. Slow flapping of wings above his head, their legs dangling from feathered thighs, flying closer than Daryl's ever seen. He turns.

"Michael!"

When the flatbed is far behind them, Michael slows down so he can hear.

"Your moniker?" Daryl's laughing, "The Mirthless."

People think the swamp is lush. But in the fall when the perennials die back and shed, it's wild and brittle: pods burst, spores dry up and crack into air, leaves shrivel and fall into the bayou. Their cycles over, beetles are floating belly up, water slaps their wings. Daryl is searching for a place so remote that the swamp birds breed there in spring, a mile-long island hidden deep in the swamp. The skiff's route follows a circuitous bayou winding obliquely from the east. The bayou leads them to a clear lake where his objective rises from its center: Cane Island, a Mecca of wild cane dotted with forests. At its northern tip, where the rookery is concealed, the passage to Cane Island is impassable, a thread of water covered by low hanging branches. Herons copulate and breed there in the spring after the heavy rains, when leap tides surge across its shore, penetrating the forest. The flooding carries their food; the sludge is teeming with frogs and crayfish. Creeping fiddler crabs—myth claims they are liars condemned to dance sideways—sidestep straight into open beaks. By summer the birds' young strut the shore in gregarious crèches, trade knowledge, and learn to fly and fend for themselves. At noon the sun is hot and hazy overhead, baking the nursery. Herons stand over their chicks, wings spread, feathers ruffled, and vibrate muscles and bones. Turning their backs to the heat, they track the sun's rays, thousands of wings flapping in unison: a squalid city of birds.

Michael docks directly across from the island's southern rim on a sandy shore in the wilderness. It's as if they're at a beach, without the blankets. The boat, half on sand, half washed by the tide, sways. Michael's dogs race into the water, churning spry to swim: a bird flies into the sky, black against the sun's white orb. Daryl strips, tossing his clothes into the boat, and asks Monique to join him, but she doesn't want Michael to see her naked.

"There's snakes in there," Michael warns. But Daryl sees the dogs splashing without fear. They bark as if calling to him, and he wades in, water lapping up his legs, the sun warming his back, and dives.

It's colder than he expected, dark and opaque. He resurfaces, the light momentarily blinding him, shakes the water from his face, and swims for the island. The world they have entered exists outside the parameters of humankind. The dogs are there, paws planted, howling from the island's shore. Light bounces off the water, birds shriek messages. Daryl can hear Michael and Monique speak; their words travel over the water, revealing their secrets to him. They ought to be more careful, Daryl thinks, his arms tossing water; the water is a prism.

"We could go anywhere we want, let Beau have the farm." That's Michael.

And Monique's contorted, "Why? What's he ever done for you, *cher*, what?"

Michael can't answer. Daryl slows down, his strokes shallow, until she goes on.

"You've always talked about Beau like we were in church. I thought I'd be meeting a saint."

She'd never even met him! Daryl rolls into a backstroke so he can see her face: it's stricken. A saint? Daryl almost shouts out loud, What the hell made you think that? The man was most likely drunk when he fucked the woman he helped make your mom, couldn't even be bothered to check the result.

Michael draws his knees into his chest and clasps them tight. "It was easy, even when he's playing here, he's someplace else. I made him up."

Daryl figures they both did. He reaches the island's shore. Stalks of wild cane prickle the soles of his feet. He can hear the dogs barking down a path through the trees, as if leading the way.

The south side of the island shelters an abandoned hunting camp, set on a hill with a line of stilted cabins overlooking the lake. Daryl climbs wooden steps up to a lopsided porch. Five more identical structures border a grassy clearing. He shakes the loose railing. Inside, bunk beds line the walls, the berths crisscrossed with hammock strings. Light beams down from a circular hole in the roof where a stovepipe had channeled smoke. The cement blocks beneath the hole are stained with ash. A breeze enters through the open door, carrying the stench of rotten fish, then dies. Back out on the porch, Daryl surveys the camp. An open-air kitchen dominates one side of the clearing. He crosses the overgrown yard and steps onto its platform: long wooden counters divide the workspace; metal basins are stacked by a brick fireplace. Daryl sniffs the grill as if he could smell the remains of crackle from duck and quail, flesh from perch and gar. The dogs come up to sit at his heels. Standing buck naked in a deserted encampment on the edge of a tangled forest and a swamp lake, Daryl does not feel exposed, nor does the word *forsaken* cross his mind: Very nice setup is what he's thinking—as far as hunting camps go. The water tank is full of last night's rain. He can hear the soft plopping as frogs, having leapt into the cistern, try to crawl up its slippery interior only to fail and slip down again. Adjacent to the clearing, an incline leads to a rickety dock that slants into the water. Just sitting here, ready and waiting for us, he concludes.

Walking back, Daryl hears Michael speaking before he sees them. Michael's mimicking Monique's voice, "We got on just fine, I fucked him, didn't I?" Then in his own voice, "That was stupid."

Monique's confidence sounds like a come-on. "That's an answer of sorts. I say, do it!"

Daryl shouts, "Hey! Of sorts? The sex was better than that."

Michael and Monique break off talking, palms shading their eyes from the sun, scanning the island's shore until they locate him.

Sunlight hits Daryl's back, shimmering off his sweat like a halo.

"I found our safe house. Bring my clothes on over."

# 7

# FAT LEROY'S CAVERN

Leroy's so fat he had to build himself a new bar so he could fit behind it. That's why it's called Fat Leroy's by Leroy's Landing. Locals quip, "Fat Leroy's crushing the landing, more like it." Fat Leroy's is a proper restaurant with a gleaming dance floor for Saturday nights. It straddles a tarred-over field across from his old place on the bayou. He still owns that shack by the levee, where he sells fishing and hunting licenses, and the overcooked hamburgers, but he spends most of his time in the big place, sitting in a custom-made high stool by the cash register, where he calls the shots, and not just liquor, because Leroy rules. Intending to keep his customers white here, too, that's what he hires. Fat Leroy's serves serious food, everything he wants to eat, fresh off the bayous and fried: shrimp, crawfish, oysters, and alligator for real. He's built himself a cavern of polished cypress walls, smooth cypress booths, beamed cypress ceiling, and carved cypress columns. Leroy's bar hugs the dining room like a bridge through a lacquered forest. His band of regulars, all local white men—farmers and laborers, small businessmen and wildcatters—are crowded around, catching the show: Beau, empty shot glass on hand, has been counting out twenty-, then ten- then five-, and now one-dollar bills. He looks up at Leroy (Leroy's big both ways) and shouts, "Three hundred and forty-four!" as if he's accomplished something. It's false pride; he's pleading.

Beau used to be, if not a member of Leroy's crowd, at least a hip appendage, the local boy made good; meaning he'd played outside of the parish (New Orleans, Baton Rouge, and Lafayette), out of state (Mobile, Houston, and Los Angeles), and once in a while up North (New York). They knew that he'd ditched them for more talented company—Black jazz musicians—whenever he could. And even then, he was tolerated by the good ol' boys because once upon a time he had signed with a famous record label. That's when he started to really mess up. And for every failure—Beau's band disbanded, he got busted and convicted for marijuana possession, his second record didn't sell, nor his third—the men he'd tried to leave behind applauded. Leroy's crew feel vindicated for their lack of ambition by Beau's failures, justified in judging him. He has always tried to escape and always lands back at Leroy's: pissed off, drunk, and arrogant.

Leroy's implacable "That covers what you owe from May and June. You still got last March to pay up on," draws snickers all around.

The sheriff is leaning all over the cash, smiling like a dog in heat. "Must've been against all those gold records he was gonna get."

Outright laughter. Among those living in the smattering of hamlets bordering the swamp, everyone's familiar with everyone else's past.

The sheriff says, "Gold record, get it? For gettin' off with coloreds!"

"Matthew, you're color-*blind*, inherited that from your

father." This finally pilfers a few chuckles. Beau pulls his snakeskin boot off. "Good thing somebody around here makes money besides you, Leroy." He shakes the cowboy boot upside down over the bar, its speckled scales catching the light. Folded bills flutter to the counter.

"Take what I owe."

Everybody respects attitude from someone in an untenable position, the laughter's softer, appreciative. This is when Michael and Daryl walk in—back from their excursion to Cane Island—on cue, it seems. Beau standing with his boot off, what's left of his little toe swathed in gauze. Leroy counting the latest installment, Michael and Daryl sidling up beside Beau, Beau whispering to Michael, "'bout time, Tonto."

There's something disturbing about Beau; even wrecked, his eyes can pin you. It's his sense of entitlement. Beau's music is his power, and he knows it: People fear talent, hate and revere those who have it. It's how you deflect that fear— whether you suffer the hate or accept the reverence—that determines your place in society. At the moment, Beau's hanging between disdain and mute respect. It could go either way. Only Daryl sees Michael slip Beau the money, but everyone around the bar can feel the shift.

Leroy's finished counting. "Still owe me, Beau."

Beau throws Michael's cash on the counter. "I was just tellin' Leroy, he could use me around here, now that I'm back. Play with the house band, liven things up."

That a boy, thinks Daryl, insult Leroy's musicians. Leroy

isn't impressed; he counts out all but a few twenties and hands these to Beau, who pockets them, disregarding the fact that they used to be Michael's.

Daryl watches Michael: he's gloating, taking care of Beau makes him feel needed.

Matthew's preoccupied, checking Daryl out. "Michael, let me buy you and your friend here a drink." Daryl recognizes him as the sheriff who was keeping an eye on Monique while patrolling Richard's.

Leroy slaps a bottle of Pearl in front of Michael—"Michael's drinks are on me, house rule"—and hands one to Daryl. "And his friend's."

Just not his daddy's, Daryl notes. He feels no obligation to introduce himself.  They'd recognize the Monroe name, but no one can place his face.

Michael's lapping up the attention. "Thanks, Leroy."

Leroy and Michael are beaming with pride, as if the fat man is Michael's lord protector. Daryl figures if Leroy wants to plant his fat ass between them and the sheriff, that's fine with him.

Beau's wavering again, this time between relief and jealousy, screaming. "You hear me, Leroy? Open up a new tab for me and my son. I'll play the first week pro bono. See what I draw, then we'll discuss my cut."

Daryl sighs; the man's relentless. Michael's shame flames up his face. The entire room rushes to his defense: "Do it Leroy, he can still play."

For Michael, Leroy softens like a shucked oyster. "One week."

In a booth, encased in cypress retreat, Michael can't take his eyes off his father. A plate of fried shrimp sits before him, untouched. Beau's slapping backs, chumming up.

"Let it go, Michael, he can take care of himself."

"Fuck you."

"Fuck me? You want to get out of this family shit or do you like runnin' everybody? Tell your sister who not to fuck, your daddy how to fight his little wars." Michael puts his beer down for that one as if to say he's had enough, but Daryl's not done: "Mr. Fixit," laughing, "our local savior."

This is Daryl's private joke, but Michael likes the comparison; he seems relieved.

"What about you? Heir apparent to nothing."

Daryl laughs. It's true. He's kept his order liquid and is nursing his beer.

Michael persists. "Why'd you come back?"

He looks beyond Michael. The sheriff's scrutinizing them, his lizard eyes half-closed in warning. "To take you away from all this."

Noland and his hunting buddies press through a side door and head for the bar.

Michael pretends not to notice them. "I mean it, what do you want?"

"Everything." Daryl thought he knew that. "Your connections. Black field labor that works for my father for next to nothing to be working with us for sky's the limit."

The sheriff's observing them so intently it's as if he can hear every word.

Daryl doesn't care. "We'll use the labor to network an operation through every bayou between here and Texas. Give them the merchandise as a loan and let them find their own market. Beats trashing cane. Once it's set up and running smoothly, I'll split. You take over, keep something for us, some for protection, and some for payoffs to the fat slugs that run this parish." He nods toward the sheriff to let him know that he's being discussed.

This is what makes Michael laugh. "They don't accept payoffs for Black people to do business around here, Daryl. They think it's beneath them. The field hands know that, they're not stupid."

Daryl glances towards the sheriff; the greedy bastard's smiling. Yes, he will. "Monique works for you, and she's not stupid."

"That's different." Michael considers Beau. The men are slapping him on the back and slurping up the drinks he's just bought them.

Daryl's clear on his facts: Michael can come and go in the Black community without condemnation, and no one among the white parishioners blames him for not knowing better, their common view: Beau's fault, he taught him wrong.

Beau's waving Michael's cash. "Leroy! Another round for my buddies here."

Michael's gaze returns to Daryl.

"Everybody wants to be somebody else, Michael. Even you."

Beau had made time to take Daryl and Michael into the swamp forests when they were thirteen for a southern initiation. Hunting was the excuse, their ability to kill wild game considered the entrance into manhood. Beau didn't exactly see it that way, but he taught them about the deer. How you have to tramp into the forest hours before dawn, climb up into the blind—a raft of wood jammed into the crook of a tree—and freeze waiting for your prey, with shots of bourbon warming you at first, then contributing to the clatter of shivering teeth. Daryl braced his limbs to be still enough to shoot slow and steady when the deer appeared. The animal smelled the mist for his scent, catching it at the same time Daryl raised his gun. Through the site, he saw nostrils flare in recognition; eyes bulged with alarm, neck twisted to flee—BLAM. When Daryl opened his eyes, dark blood had soaked the deer's golden hide, and the animal had crumpled onto the tall grass. He climbed down from the blind, put his rifle to the deer's head, and shot it out of its misery. It made him sick; the innocent eyes dull with pain, straining to see its killer, whimpering for its life. When, a week later, Michael's turn came, he shot as if he were half-crazed, gored his deer but refused to see the damage. Beau made them give thanks to the dead deer, the deer's progenitors, and then—this was Beau's own interpretation—

the dawn and the night before the dawn. He smeared sticky blood from the animals' wounds onto the boys' cheeks and foreheads. Stinking ritual, but Daryl believes it did make a man of him: he doesn't look back, does what he has to do, and never allows himself to think of the consequences; they're too painful.

After Daryl went away to school and was back some years later for a holiday, he learned the real reason for Beau's two-year absence from their childhood, which had been camouflaged by Beau's sporadic disappearances throughout their youth. He'd been sent upriver for possession. Conceit had ruled his judgment; Beau had let himself get caught flaunting a few reefers. Blowing the offense out of all proportion, the good ol' boys sent Beau to jail because he hadn't paid them enough respect. Daryl has never discussed this with Michael, and Michael's never mentioned it, but in Daryl's opinion, Michael bows so low to the ruling caste that his ass hits the sky, then does anything he wants, wreaking far more damage than his daddy ever did.

# 8

# The Gulf

Billowing fog rolls over a tumultuous sea. Unlike the sedentary waters in the bayous, those in the Gulf of Mexico are imperceptibly swift. Perverse winds blast the night, shoving atmosphere and sea spray north and west. Out of the darkness an oil platform, floating on the sea, groans. Its shaft pounds as loud as the wind howls, its warning lights dim in the fog; rafts buoy its mass, tires buffer its perimeter. Anxious men, soft and obscure in the fog, tread scaffolding and attend to rotating gears. A shifting group of the temporarily employed, these men occupy two worlds. For fourteen days the riggers pace the confines of their steel island to eat, sleep, and work. And when their two-week shift is over, they ferry back to land and families where they sleep, drink, and copulate, and fourteen days later, return to the sea.

Above the kitchen, seagulls swoop between rigging, shrieking. No men patrol the lowest ramp. The birds dive into swollen garbage bags floating off the galley, tearing at scraps from the night's meal. One of the riggers, hunched like an owl, descends a ladder toward the waves. Men are easy to lose in the dark. He clings to the receiving dock, hissing to the winds, *"Cuidado! Aqui! Sigue el sonido de la campana. Tírame la cuerda!"* And as if from a nether world, voices respond, not from the late shift treading the rig's deck, but outside their circumference, from the bow of a shrimp boat, *"Puedes ver? Agárrala."* Enigmatic the way the ship undulates in and out of light, its dark hull tossed by the sea, creaking in the wind.

This is the drop-off point, where Daryl suspects but has yet to find. Address—half a mile, a mile, could be three miles off the Louisiana coast. One of over 4,000 rigs rocking somewhere between Mexico and Louisiana—identified by company number, the company having been registered with an omnipresent title, The Gulf.

The rumors Daryl had heard in New Orleans excited him: an uncharted drug line from drop-offs made on the rigs, moving up via the bayous and comprised of small maverick operations controlled by no one in particular. While smuggling contraband up into Louisiana's twisting bayous was nothing new, drop-offs from Mexican or American boats directly to men working on the offshore oil rigs were, in Daryl's opinion, an ingenious development. Any boat unloading meals, machine parts, or riggers whisked to land by ferries and motorboats, circumvented the Coast Guard, who were on the lookout for speedboats darting from the Gulf into the Louisiana bayous, not the rigs' suppliers, or men returning home. Once in the bayous, a local carrier who knew the waters would be impossible to track. The vulnerable area for a drug transfer was within the three-mile border zone before the coast, the area now occupied by the rigs. When drug enforcement would catch on and have the men in place to do something about it was only a matter of time. Daryl's intention is to use this slip in time.

Mining oil at sea is a risky, dangerous business. Daryl likes the combination of one risky endeavor supporting another covert one and temporarily lessening its risk in the process, a situation so ripe with contradiction that he gets a rush just thinking about it. The transfer is already occurring; Michael's one of the links, but Daryl has yet to discover his source. Michael's given up all pertinent information one square inch at a time: how much cash Daryl needs to make a substantial purchase and to bring it.

He's washed and waxed his Ford Bronco and put on clean black jeans for the transaction, but he hasn't told Daryl who else is involved or where the two of them are going. Daryl's sprawled over the passenger seat in anticipation, and Michael's cruising the back roads of the Atchafalaya swamp as if all he means to do is show off its attractions. They're driving past wooden shacks that seem to be tossed helter-skelter through the trees: sedentary waters pass under the floorboards; washbasins litter the front yards; stilted porches double as docks with rowboats left by the stairs. The sun is setting when the truck approaches a tumbledown farm by the edge of the swamp and Daryl sees a blonde girl-child who is so incongruous with her surroundings, so pale in complexion that he thinks, Apparition. Delicate hair tangles past her knees. She's dressed in immaculate white—a bleach-worn frock laced with blue ribbon—and leading a kid goat to the river's edge. Michael's familiar with her routine and stops the truck as if he meant to meet her. But the child comes up to Daryl's open window. Her breath hits his neck; its gurgle mingles with the goat's hoarse gasping. The child's nails are long.

Michael explains, "She's a seer. When a girl-child is born sick, the parents promise her to the Virgin Mary. Never cut her hair or nails, dress her in the virgin's colors. They think it'll cure her."

"What the hell, they never hear of sanatoriums?"

"And in return, she heals others, foresees things, answers prayers."

Daryl sees it, the pale consumptive eyes and sanguine cheeks. He searches his pockets for his wallet. "That's ridiculous, it should be against the damned law—she's just a kid. I'll cover the medical costs."

Michael laughs. "You're the one bein' ridiculous. It's their faith—ask her a question."

Daryl's so distraught, he can't find his billfold; all he comes up with is crystallized sugar. "Sweetheart, do you want some candy?"

Michael interjects, "He wants his future."

"No, I don't. I'll find it soon enough, anyway." Daryl can't stop looking at her blue irises, almost white, opaque. Reflected in the truck's side mirror is his own visage, his sunglasses reflecting her face.

Michael's adamant, "Ask her for me, will you?"

Daryl grins at the child. "Come on up here."

The child steps onto the truck's running board; her fingers use his door for ballast. Her eyes are not those of a child, but her dimpled cheeks and the sweet tilt of her head suggest innocence. Daryl places a protective arm around her shoulders and whispers, "You know what happens to everybody, *cher*?"

The child nods yes.

Daryl strokes her arm, thinking scrawny and delicate. "Can you keep a secret?"

The girl twists her head no.

"You want me to tell him?"

The child shakes her head.

Daryl turns to Michael, whispering so that she can't hear. "They die. That's what's going to happen."

Michael shifts the clutch. "Fine, Sherlock, forget it. Let's go."

The air cools without the sun. They'd left the Bronco under an old rail bridge and switched to the motorboat Michael had hidden at a nearby dock. A great blue heron spied them leaving the cove and rose from its perch. Michael cut the boat lights; the moon was bright. At night, swamp trees blot into ink, their limbs waving. Creatures with predatory eyes prowl the forests and wetlands. Daryl's finished off a line; he always samples the merchandise. This coke of Michael's is fraught with an edge so that he can't tell what's in him or what's surrounding him. He feels jumpy; false fears gnaw at him. Sounds amplify, a creeping eruption that echoes in the air: the murky silence of the hunted, the victorious shriek of the hunter. Ghosts are drawn to swamps; their whispers roil over the waters like furies. Wings rub shrill organs; voices, like children's, call from the trees. Black water beetles dive-bomb his head; croaking frogs surround the boat. This is not the edge Daryl expected. He's not sure if it's Michael or his connections that are trifling with him, but there's something smug about the way Michael's eyes dart from Daryl's twitchy discomfort to the night ahead that stack the odds toward him. Daryl's certain: Michael's showing off by cutting the shit with speed, as if he were only a customer, so he flashes his gear, a .45, and aims it in Mike's direction.

"Mike, look what I got."

Michael turns white. But Daryl's mood flips, and he's laughing uncontrollably, every gesture is a private joke. The gun dangles from his hand, the boat rocks, and he almost falls backward into the bayou giggling, but catches himself.

Michael seems back in time, one hand gripping the boat's rim. "Are you nuts?" His voice skips through the swamp, as if he were calling to someone.

The laughter rising to Daryl's nostrils turns to bile. "You never know who you can trust. Me for instance, isn't that what you really wanted to ask that girl-child? If you can trust me?" Spite's ugly, it crawls up Daryl's face and collapses into resentment, but he can't stop. "And Monique. You don't trust her now that I've fucked her. You don't have to trust somebody to fuck 'em. You think I trust her? Or you?" Daryl's spitting. "Monique wanted to fuck me. You want to fuck Monique?"

"Shut up Daryl, and hand me the gun or you'll get us both killed."

Daryl swings the pistol, whistling Dixie.

Michael turns off the motor. The boat drifts toward a copse of trees, witchy shadows are moving through the branches.

It's true, Daryl thinks, I'm out of control. But the laughter comes back, less insistent this time, releasing him. "Because I do believe we'll be meeting some real live rednecks, and if we run into trouble, you can save us with those big strong arms of yours." A giggle now, more a hiccup, and a flamboyant flip of his wrist. "Oh Michael, this is so excitin'."

Daryl's calmed, his induced frenzy has passed, but he vows not to forget the episode, he's storing it for later remuneration. Moving against the current, they've reached the brackish waters before the sea. The marshlands are less spectacular and quieter than the swamp; cattails swish, miniature waves lap, but otherwise an uncanny silence reigns. Daryl sits, legs up on the rail of the boat, aiming at nothing, cocking and uncocking the pistol just for the rhythm of it. Michael's concerned; a loaded gun displayed means loaded intentions, but he doesn't want to provoke another frenzy. Daryl's aware of his quandary, that's what he likes about Michael, his fatalism. The blue heron glides by on salty air.

"Someone's followin' us." Daryl stops his game.

"That's a bird."

A motorboat drifts out of the night. There's radar on its bow, a man with an automatic rifle sitting at its stern, and another man steering from the helm. The one hunched like an owl howls, *"Hijo de puta,"* and aims his automatic at Daryl.

"Give me the gun, Daryl." For once, Daryl obeys him. Michael tries to explain, "Thought we were being followed."

The boats drift so close they knock. Noland, Joseph Monroe's foreman, is the boat's pilot. Daryl could have told Noland that working for his father as a lackey didn't pay enough. Michael's tying a line from their boat onto Noland's stern.

"Small world, Daryl. Get in."

That's Noland, yet again, whose world, Daryl knows, will always be smaller than his. The man's a necessary blight, a spoke in his well-oiled wheel of velocity, the next key to the puzzle. He calms himself with an unspoken promise: it's a temporary alliance.

Noland's careening his boat through grassy waters, contorting their trail so that Daryl can't keep track, but Michael's noting the turns and tracing the wake. The one toting the automatic is Jorge, a dark stocky man who understands almost no English. It hardly matters, the boat's moving too fast for talk. They ride a choppy path of air and water, no difference between the night and the river, both contain the same darkness. Up ahead, a spot of light moves in the haze and then vanishes. Noland cuts the motor and steers, drifting in its direction.

They're up to it before it takes shape, the stark bulk of an abandoned houseboat rising and falling in the channel. The others clamber onto the deck, but Daryl's inert, the water flowing beneath his feet feels constant, even as the motorboat rocks. He's looking for whoever doused the light. Noland believes fear is keeping Daryl still, but fear eats souls, and Daryl's too ravenous to share his.

Noland spits, "I'm waitin', rich boy."

Let him, Daryl decides, wait all he wants, a few more gray cells and Noland wouldn't have to pretend he was running things, he would be. Power exists in the first person only, which is what Daryl's searching for. His eyes scan the dark, he can feel a presence stalking them, but it won't light. Michael's gone inside with the others. Daryl steps onto the deck and follows them across the threshold.

He examines the room: swollen wooden slats from floor to ceiling, boarded windows, a musty old cot, but no human smells—a stone-cold kerosene stove. Michael hunches his shoulders, and Jorge hugs his automatic rifle. The first door they'd tried was stuck shut from the damp; the one they entered through hangs half open.

Noland is still pretending he's in charge. He lights a hurricane lamp. "I'm still waitin', rich boy."

Man's only good for one line, why bother? Daryl stalls. Mimicking a minstrel, he contorts his chest into obsequious search, pats his pockets, and then slaps them as if to beat out the truth. "Gee Noland, I forgot the cash."

Noland's bug-eyed with fear, and Michael's struck dumb.

Jorge growls, "Motherfucker."

Daryl doesn't take it personally but pulls out his pockets' linings for all to see and shrugs: a public display of penury.

"I'm real-ly sorry."

This time, Jorge's "Motherfucker" does sound personal; he's aiming his rifle at Daryl's head. Michael surprises all of them by jumping to Daryl's rescue, spinning the .45 into Jorge's ear. The détente's breathless, but Daryl's performance has worked, the door comes unglued, and a snarling force collects in the light: raven black hair, a pale almost feminine face—it's the aquiline nose because his eyes are ice gray and his body's rock hard. The captain of some inconsequential vessel, that's what he was born to; his hands and chest are muscular from pulling ropes.

"You are a crazy fool."

They all back off, Michael included.

"Like to see who I'm dealing with."

The captain opens his arms; it's not a gesture of supplication. "Let's go."

Daryl throws two bricks of cash retrieved from each rubber boot. They land with a thud at Noland's feet. Noland scoops up the bills like he's about to sit, but rises immediately, offering them to the captain.

What Daryl would really like to see is Noland crawl.

The captain expects it. "Count it."

Daryl asks, "You have a name?"

"Arevan. Come on over here."

Daryl steps carefully towards Arevan's razor-toothed grin. He glances over at Michael, who actually seems relaxed. They've got time; Noland loses track counting the cash and starts over again.

"I said, Come 'ere."

When Daryl's up to him, Arevan draws a knife across his own index finger and offers Daryl his blood. "Suck it," jabbing the bloody digit between Daryl's lips.

Daryl licks the salty fluid with his tongue, eyes on Arevan's, and sends him a kiss.

Arevan grabs Daryl's finger, slices the skin and sucks the blood, his tongue rolling red between his lips. Wiping his mouth, he says, "You saw, learned, and heard nothing. Or I kill you."

Well, Daryl concludes, at least he's demonstrative.

Later that night they celebrated. Daryl and Michael blew into Richard's numb with laughter. They danced until closing time; bumping asses each time they collided with each other on the dance floor and drank two bottles of champagne. Music blurred, light circled, came into focus, and retreated into darkness. Daryl spotted Kyle, Monique's acquaintance from the cane fields. Kyle, sitting straight and immobile on the sidelines, mixed with no one: he was too busy watching Michael and Daryl make fools of themselves. Daryl pointed him out to Michael, who knew him by sight. Daryl would have asked him to dance just to see if the man could laugh but changed his mind. Instead, he produced his card, embossed black lettering on ivory stock: "Daryl Monroe, Entrepreneur," no address, no phone number. He wrote "Cane Island" on its reverse side.

Sauntering up to Kyle, Daryl whispered, "I'd talk now but I'm too drunk."

# 9

# The Library

Daryl's waking hours have slipped from day to night. Long after midnight, he's inspecting his family's library in darkness. He opens the French doors leading to the garden but draws the curtains closed to conceal his presence. Silk drapes flirt with lazy winds blowing in from the south. Rifling through his father's files confound the puzzle. Contracts and deeds are coded by Arabic numerals, but what the numbers stand for, whether they refer to current or past transactions, Daryl cannot determine. His father's business dealings are opaque; his oil wells, also identified by number, have no recorded coordinates with which to figure their location. Topographical maps of the Gulf hang over an entire wall, but they're unmarked. Among the swarm of rigs erected off the Louisiana coast, Daryl assumes that Noland and Arevan are using the ones his father owns. Why else would Noland continue to work for Joseph Monroe, unless he needed access to his rigs?

The telex prints out world news—Daryl reads the scroll with his flashlight's round beam: Workers are on strike in Poland; a Socialist has been sworn in as the premier of France; Iranians are dragging their drug addicts into the street and shooting them on the spot. The local weather report follows: unseasonably warm. The red light blinking on the phone indicates that his father's awake upstairs, conversing with someone in another time zone. He sweeps the room with his flashlight; its beam darts, catching glassy-eyed stuffed birds standing on antique tables and shelves lined with books. Knowledge, like a code, must be deciphered. Daryl used to break the spines of books. Books with broken spines lay flat, pages didn't rush forward when the story began, and the gravity of what was written didn't pull the rest to completion before the he got there. He'd rip the corners and eat the paper—as a child, he believed eating its words made the story a part of him, marked his place. There was nothing inviolable about his mother's books; they were there to be consumed.

He's searching the shelves for the last book he read to her. Her volumes have been sorted by author and then arranged by subject, so compulsive an accounting that it unnerves him, until he finds the frayed copy of *Metamorphoses*. Its swollen paper is ripe with mildew; its leather binding curves into his palm. Before settling into the couch by the fireplace, he pours himself a shot of bourbon. He wants to find in Ovid's pages the counterpart to the great blue heron he saw in the Atchafalaya. Animals can be omens, and birds always portend an incident.

He hadn't forgotten, but perhaps because of his mother's sickness, he'd been careful in his choices for her, *Metamorphoses* recounts tale after tale of violent bloodletting and scandal: Circe wanted Picus to mount her, and when he rebuffed her advances for the love of his wife, she turned him into a woodpecker. Opposite of a cuckold, Daryl imagines.

Tereus raped Philomela, then cut off her wagging tongue so she couldn't tell on him. Consequently, he was tricked by her sister—his wife—into eating their son. The revenge occurred at a Bacchanalian feast, whereupon clawing for revenge in his grief, he changed into a hoopoe. Daryl heads for the dictionary and finds that hoopoes are not lore as he had thought but indigenous to the Old World.

Courtly Daedalion, seeking his own death after his daughter's murder, was transformed into a hawk so he could prey on others and in his grief, multiply theirs. Poetic justice, Daryl believes, but it's not what he's looking for. Ovid traces the lineage of the wading and diving birds, whose preserved corpses crowd the library, back to two lovers, Lucifer's son Ceyx, and the Wind's daughter, Alcyone. The night Ceyx drowned at sea, Alcyone saw the disaster in a dream and ran from their bed to the shoreline where she sprouted wings, skimming over the waves to embrace her lover's corpse. The gods changed them both into long-necked divers. Irritated by the sentimentality, Daryl flips the pages. Sirens scoured the earth looking for Persephone, and to accommodate their searching the seas, the Gods turned their arms into wings as well. Daryl snorts: could have just told them, Persephone's in Hell. Ascalaphus found her there sucking a pomegranate and tattled on her, sealing both their fates. Furious, her mother, Demeter, tossed fire into his face; he shrieked so long that he became a screech owl.

Finally, at the end of Ovid's tales, Daryl finds Ardea,

an abandoned city destroyed by fire. The heron rose from its ashes, beat its embers with gray-blue wings, and lived on sweet sap and incense, smoky fumes and myrrh. This is what Daryl wants; something that falls in line with his ambitions. As far as omens go, it's what he hopes, and, yes, prays for—to rise from Cane Island's isolation and recover some of what he's lost.

There exists in the library another ancient text, one that was not recorded by Ovid and which Daryl has not read. It describes a city of birds built in the air between Heaven and Earth. A city-state from where the birds intended to charge a toll for the passage of man's prayers to the gods. Cranes treaded air and dazzling sky to bring the foundations' stones. Storks, purple lapwings, and silver water birds brought water to the air. Pelicans hauled mortar in their beaks; geese used their webbed feet as trowels; ducks carried bricks two by two in buckets; swallows brought straw. And when the city was complete, the birds divided into squadrons. The sky whizzed and whirred with them. Falcons, hawks, and buzzards searched for men to tax. No plea for rain, prayers for vengeance or deliverance were to pass to the gods without their intervention. The birds planned to catch the fumes of incense, the offerings of sizzling blood and smoky flesh, and hold the gifts until they were paid in kind. If man refused, they would retaliate by eating their crops, pecking at the eyes of their livestock, or defecating in their water supply. But man outsmarted the birds and took over their domain. The birds were not the masters of their fate. Oh, they acted as messengers between heaven and earth, but those messages still ascended to the gods with sacrifices meant to benefit, not the birds, but their rulers.

## CANE ISLAND

Birds surround Cane Island; ibis glide into its forest, heron stalk the lake. Daryl, Monique, and Michael have become its sole human inhabitants, establishing their safe house at the abandoned hunting camp. If the island and its compound are owned, who possesses it cannot be found in any court record. Daryl has settled for squatters' rights. Michael arrived early to repair one of the cabins: he swept the spider webs and rodent nests from its four corners and tacked mosquito nets onto the roof that drape over broken glass windows to the earth. The entire camp's dilapidated, overrun with swarms of mosquitoes. Hazy clouds of the bloodsuckers infest the sky, a final scourge before winter brings about their demise. The shallow bayou leading to the island's lake is impossible to navigate with anything larger than a skiff and will remain so until spring's torrential rains. Even then, it is so remote that only trappers remember the route. The lake that serves as a natural moat and the impenetrable forest at its north fortify the island. Burning cedar torches surround the open-air kitchen. Michael's afraid the dark billows rising from their hideout like signals will be noticed. But Daryl has decided it doesn't matter, the mosquitoes are tormenting him; he's dousing himself with witch hazel to draw the poison and claims to be weak from blood loss. If anyone sees the smoke and is curious enough to drop by, he has a cover: they're starting a frog farm—

croaks echo all over the island to prove it—raising plump, juicy legs for restaurants in the area and beyond.

Daryl is, in fact, starting a cottage industry. They're chopping blocks of cocaine, not with razor blades but with butcher knives; that's how much they scored, cutting it with Ex-Lax. Daryl likes the way it sounds, concise and lazy. They're using the laxative's infant dosage so that their customers will be relieved rather than inhibited. The cabin's a cocoon of white dust that's clouding the air and entering their pores, their nerves narcotized. Neither Michael nor Daryl will leave the camp until the shipment has been divided and stashed. The three of them are working as if on speed, noisy sky and freaky branches swaying above the fire hole over their heads.

The birds feed at five a.m. sharp, squawking and jabbering to wake the dead. They skim the lake and drop crustaceans on the rooftop to crack the shells, a code of sorts that lasts for hours. Daryl and Michael are numb and silly with lack of sleep. Monique's skin is veiled with white powder, golden honey-colored under the dope. Daryl licks her shoulder, bitter as a root, and sucks at her arm. She pushes him away, laughing, but they both feel like a shower. Monique washes his neck with her tongue, working her way to his chest, stopping at his belly to tease. Michael's stone-still, so lonely that he's about to cry out. Daryl takes pity and tackles him, holding him down while Monique licks his cheeks; then Daryl outdoes her, nipping at Michael's neck, slurping at his throat.

Michael's caught. He opens up, laughing, "No," then tickled, folds his legs and contracts, filling their hands with his weight. He rolls out of their grasp to flop from side to side. "Stop it, get off of me."

They're not on him. The three of them are gulping with laughter, limbs flung out to the four corners, when Kyle enters. They didn't hear him coming, there was no sign from the dogs. He manifests in front of them, eyes like a hawk's. Kyle, the light-skinned Black man Monique snagged at the sideshow in the cane fields, the one watching Michael and me at Richards, Daryl assesses the situation: the one who turns Monique on—well, him *and* me. If Kyle agrees to join them, all the labor that Daryl needs—runners and dealers— will follow. Kyle's preoccupied with Monique. She's arrogant in her dishabille, a turn-on for any man. Monique looks from Kyle to Daryl with fear as if Daryl's making her choose, but it's Kyle who's asking. Daryl rises to the occasion, an ingratiating host it would seem, but it's to get a better view of the man. Kyle doesn't need an invitation; he sprawls himself over a chair by the mound of coke and helps himself to a sample with Daryl's butcher knife, snorting it up his nose. Licking the knife clean, staring back at Daryl. Daryl expects a welt of blood to flower up around his tongue, but Kyle's good with knives: no fear, no blood. He rubs his gums and smacks his lips, savoring the tingling of his tongue and the clogging in his nostrils. Not greedy, notes Daryl, discerning.

Kyle leans back to hear what Daryl has to say.

"We're lookin' for distributors."

"You want me to sell this for you?" Kyle's laughter comes easy and full until it stops. "Make your own profit off my brothers and sisters, ones who work your family's fields as if they were migrant labor—if you can." Shrugging Michael's way, "He don't do half bad. Let him keep doin' it."

And the Lord said, *Vengeance is mine*, Daryl muses, I don't think so. Out loud he says, "That's not all that buys; white customers line up for it, too."

Kyle acts amused. "You want me to sell this to *white* folk?" Then sours again, "Like I said, you do it."

Daryl persists. "Buying from a Black man's more illicit, more exciting, makes the high more authentic. White folk think y'all have better drugs and better sex. Not that that's necessarily true."

Kyle smiles. "How the hell you know what we have?"

"I don't. That's the point." Daryl glances over Monique's way; her smile's an alliance, but his disclosure is for Kyle. "What's illicit's considered dangerous. Danger gets the juices pumping; swamps the prosaic. Thrill's synonymous with sex. Transforms good ol' boys into dragon slayers, giggling girls into screaming women. The more illicit the purchase, the sexier the drug. I'm asking you to work it with me, perpetuate the myth." Daryl smiles, "Thrill us."

Kyle's laugh again, laced with anger, low and succinct. "Used to be, forty Black men got hung from the forty trees that lined Canal Street every time a white boy got scared his dick wasn't big enough. Now a man just gets beaten to death or rots on death row."

Monique's pride jumps up her back. Daryl catches disdain in her eyes and it's for him.

Michael chimes in: "Sheriff calls me any time there's a problem. Let's us know in advance so we can clean up and clear out."

From the pirates to the bootleggers to the Cuban cigar smugglers to the drug dealers, the local law has always stepped back. Which is how Kyle knows Michael's claim to be true.

Daryl needs his highs often and winning gives him one. Kyle's looking at Monique as if he intends to take her back with him, and she's holding her breath. So Daryl leaves her to him. Nothing dramatic, he just walks to the other end of the room and folds his arms, as if he doesn't care—she can stay or go. Monique feels the alternative. Where would Kyle take her? Back to some brick ranch house with clean sheets on the bed and a new refrigerator in its kitchen but trapped under its linoleum is filthy detritus and a warped plywood floor.

Daryl says, "No reason why white men should be the only ones to benefit from selling to white clientele. But you need us because you're not equipped; you got no capital and you're too hostile. The sheriff intervenes to work with Michael; he doesn't want to work with you. Our protection covers your ass."

Daryl's back on top, because Monique tosses her head, dismissing Kyle. They watch his departure through the scrim. The dogs are chasing iridescent dragonflies. The insects hover as if motionless. Kyle is deep in thought, daydreaming himself to the dock, stepping around piles of crawfish traps, then registering the two new skiffs moored in the lake with their bright, silver bows raised to the sky and their sterns adorned with the fastest motors money can buy. His weathered dinghy bobs at the dock. The soft hum of his motor recedes, and he's gone, back to contemplate Daryl's proposal. Which isn't entirely true; he's accepted it. Daryl can see the resignation in the slump of his shoulders.

Out in the boats, submerging the crawfish traps along channels and coulees, hiding those that contain waterproof cases stuffed with contraband among the tangled oak and cypress roots, Michael and Daryl pilot their skiffs in tandem, Michael leading the way. The swamp envelops them, a mist shrouding the water, the land and the sky. No up or down, no horizon, no ground, they float. Trees emerge from the mist and vanish as soon as they pass their branches. Birds fly out of the murky gray and fade away. The purr of their motors holds the spell. A white sail flutters before Daryl's eyes, radiant through the mist, it's an ibis, a hieroglyph of spread wings, lingering for an instant. The obscurity of Daryl's home eludes everything but some atavistic longing, and yet, in its midst, he is content with the pleasure of the torpid current under his boat, the tingling fog watering his arms, an ecstatic bird's caw over the soft swish of his line, and the sharp impression of wire on his fingers as he thrusts an empty crawfish trap into the gray waters, instigating its slow plunge. The trap sucks in water and sinks to muddy silt along the banks, awaiting its catch. Daryl wraps its wire trace, tagged with yellow and blue plastic ribbons, around the root and leaves it sticking up from the trap like a flag.

Guiding his skiff from one mapped location to the next, Daryl leans toward jutting roots, and scaring water bugs and small rodents off their meals, hides another crayfish trap in the entanglement, this one filled with contraband in a waterproof case. He marks each location on his chart. In this way, he means to keep Cane Island clean in case of search and seizure, open for meetings and monetary collection but closed to the actual transfer of drugs, except for the hours spent cutting and packing. All transactions will start by releasing a trap's location and its tag colors in exchange for collateral. Any disruption to business, a bust or an indiscretion, will be contained by this dispersion. Each pick-up constitutes a separate transaction.

Daryl and Michael travel obscure channels, leaving behind maypoles of significance. Traps for future deals are wired to tree roots, branches, and telephone poles, each line decorated with fluttering plastic ribbons. A family's colors are analogous to a coat-of-arms: the contents of the traps will not be tampered with or stolen. A man's catch is sacred in the Atchafalaya swamp. Daryl feels no guilt: He believes ingesting drugs is the closest he's come to God. There is no difference to him between the sustenance food provides and the dreams his drugs procure. The swamp's mist curls up his nostrils, fills his mouth. His past exists in this haze;

it haunts him; he inhales its vapors. Intangible, this breath, for he can't hold it long enough to remember; it wavers and once exhaled, returns to vapor.

When the silver motorboats are empty of cages, Michael spins his boat in place until Daryl catches up to him. Grinning in satisfaction, Michael guns his motor. Daryl chases after him, his bow flying into a path of waves, a froth of resistance that tosses his skiff up toward the sky and back again, his helm thudding down onto water. Michael turns under I-10, the causeway that spans the swamp. Daryl accelerates, following him into a channel bordered by the parallel pilings supporting the causeway. Rising from the water, the columns frame a seemingly infinite tunnel, a mirror to another universe. The tunnel is hypnotic, leading either to eternity or back to their camp, depending upon which they hit first. Michael glances back at Daryl, laughing from the high of it. He weaves his boat between the pilings at a reckless speed, thread the needle or crash into cold gray cement—live or die. Daryl grins in recognition; tempting mortality makes them immortal. He races Michael back to camp.

Kyle has joined them. It took him just forty-eight hours to return with his answer. The animosity between Daryl and Kyle has been stifled; their mutual jealousy, if not turning into admiration, is at least in check. Michael contacted his runners; Kyle spread the word among the appropriate settlements. Prospective dealers, looking for a change in their economic status, have lined up for consideration. There's more interest than Daryl had hoped for—more he's afraid, than Parish residents could ever handle without overdosing. He's situated himself in the yard by the camp's outdoor kitchen, his feet up on a table and his account book open, interviewing prospective "merchants," as he calls them, and collecting collateral from those he and Michael approve. People's meager earnings and inheritances are piled on the table: a wad of cash, two gold watches, one pearl necklace, a wedding band, and one deed that Michael's examining. The frown on his face tells Daryl he's reticent. When isn't he? Daryl muses; Michael's been ruthless all day.

The deed's owner, dark as earth, says, "It be very fine land. Under water, comes with fishing rights."

Daryl decides. "Sure, why not?"

Michael says, "Go on in the back, see my sister."

They have to swear on the Bible. Monique would draw blood, but Daryl insists that the mosquitoes are doing enough damage. He glances into the shaded kitchen: the initiate, one palm on the King James version, the other palm raised to the east, is trying his damndest not to look at Monique, repeating after her, "saw, learned, heard—"Monique shouts, "Nothing."

"Nothing."

And the part Monique enjoys most, "Otherwise kill me."

"Otherwise kill me. Amen."

Two bony, eager brown men of eighteen and nineteen,

Percy and Skinner, are the last in line, Kyle's cousins from Erath. "This here's their family's place, they don't need no other collateral. They'll be workin' with us."

"Skinner?" It's a question no one answers. "This," Daryl points to the ground beneath his feet, "is your family's hunting camp?"

Skinner laughs. "This ain't no hunting camp."

Daryl shrugs, "Very nice location, Skinner, right smack in the center of the food chain."

"My mother's people made turpentine."

He might have known the place had a history. Moonshine. "This public knowledge?" is what Daryl asks.

"Only my family and the birds ever found this place. Surprised you did."

"Why'd they quit?"

"Prohibition quit."

Good enough. Daryl asks, "How come they call you Skinner?"

"I'm the king, fastest frog skinner on the bayou."

Daryl laughs. They will lease the camp from Skinner, harvest the crawfish, and farm the frogs, which is precisely how he had planned to legitimize their presence on the island to begin with.

# 11

# The Discovery

What you inherit is who you are. Daryl has inherited no possessions, but he does not allow himself to believe that this means he is no one. He has other attributes: the character and reputation of his matriarchal line; accomplishments and sins, his and his family's; how he dreams at dawn or wakes in twilight; how the moon hangs like a horn over his shoulder; the way he walks into a room and holds his pride. Daryl's gaze pans across the harvested cane fields. Field hands are burning the last of the refuse. Flames bark at air; ashes fall like snow beneath the sun, its orb high and hazy. Daryl has inherited no possessions, but this does not mean that he is no one. Now, on the other hand, in Daryl's opinion, it most certainly applies to Noland the middleman. A man who intercepts tangible assets, neither buying nor selling, but stepping into a transaction to collect and live off the labor of others. Daryl's mind fills with disgust as he watches Noland parade about his mother's fields acting like he's the boss, coordinating the last of the harvest into a walkie-talkie. Daryl turns from the parlor windows and stumbles into a bathroom, where he throws up in the sink. The gold-flecked wallpaper does nothing to alleviate his nausea. Washing his face and slicking back his hair, Daryl studies himself in the mirror and sees wrinkles he's too young to have. He's weary from sampling too many samples, but his Hermès tie is straight, his white shirt's handmade and pressed, and, he sighs in relief, his bone structure can support a truckload of sin. Daryl pulls back all expression from his face and does a final appraisal. Deadpan eyes reveal nothing, and that bone structure ought to carry him miles before his flesh sags.

When Daryl enters the library, his father is at his desk pouring over account books. Checking the map of the Gulf coast on the wall, he sees with satisfaction the little red pins sticking into its surface marking the locations of offshore wells; it is a map that was hanging in full view the night of his search, but the pins were missing. Clocks and telex tick and spew, red lights blink. Fresh, white camellias have been encased, and the glassy-eyed birds, claws grasping, moth-eaten wings spread, stand motionless. Daryl says nothing; this constitutes the game between father and son: who will acknowledge whom first. He peruses the bookshelves for something to read, the Ovid's where he left it. The book rests easily in his palm, its pages eager to flip.

Joseph interrupts. "Last time we spoke, you said you were never coming back. I thought that was a promise."

Daryl leafs through the book. "Nah, just a wish."

"Dragging some colored girl through the swamps. Very seedy, boy."

Daryl starts and then realizes that this is a reference to their run-in with the hunters, and that Noland must have told him. Daryl puts the book down. "Jealous?"

"Don't make me laugh."

Daryl starts perusing the map, studying the locations of the red pins. Not to be too obvious, he produces an explanation. "She's Beau Duvet's daughter."

"Hell then, Beau Duvet! Take your pleasure where you want, Daryl, but don't go mistaking it with pride."

Joseph doesn't understand. Daryl turns to tell him. "My pleasure is my pride."

"Why don't you leave here; you'll be goin' anyway. I'll pay you."

"Thought I'd try working in the family business. Something on one of our oil platforms."

"My oil wells. What's mine stays mine and will never be yours."

Daryl winces involuntarily. "Noland ever do anything for you on the rigs?"

"Once in a while. You want his job, be my messenger boy?"

"All expenses paid?" Daryl glances at the maps as if he's interested, he is.

"To Morgan City, exciting center of nothing?"

That's the center, where they ship out, all the pins point to it. "Not particularly." Daryl is memorizing the names: Dulac, Vermilion, Calcasieu, and Cameron.

"Noland has proven to be responsible."

Daryl's engrossed. "I'll bet."

"In my day, I did everything; played around with Beau and his kind, did his drugs, fucked with anybody I wanted. But I had priorities, I knew when to put it aside."

Daryl's done. "Was that before or after mother died?"

"You weren't even here, your mother died in my arms."

This is too much. "Because you never let her leave when she got sick, get the care she needed! She could have gone to Houston or New York. You wouldn't take her because you wouldn't leave here!"

"That's a lie. She wanted to stay here, with me."

"She wanted to *die* here with you; elsewhere she could have lived." The air is stifling, the fire in the hearth burning day and night, the dust from the books and the taxidermy. Daryl never meant to get this upset. He feels like a child.

Back in the bathroom, the gold-flecked wallpaper, his sweaty face in the mirror, and the burning fields out the window float. He snorts the rest of his supply. Daryl does drugs to escape: anguish, inertia, boredom…but what he's come to understand is that drugs are no escape, just a stay of execution. He has a favorite joke: What did the death-row inmate say as they strapped him into the electric chair? "I'd rather be fishin'." Daryl needs drugs, but he expects no mercy. He's searching for ecstasy the way memory searches for paradise. Love is hopeless—it sends him plunging, like falling in a dream, panic gripping his heart. Sex gets him there for a while, but that release is a surrender. Daryl wants release with no surrender. Birds fly to soar and that's where he's happiest. He lives with an emptiness he can't fill, momentum his only relief, illicit drugs his compulsion, and the destruction of all competitors his triumph.

Outlaw, maverick, cowboy, wildcat: he loves these words, their all-American swagger, their independence, and their aspiration. Cane Island is his outlaw station, manned by Black cowboys with their own lilts and reasons for standing guard with a gun. Three weeks in business, and what was meant to function as a way station has become home. Each time he has to leave the island for supplies, or business, or a wider selection of personal drugs, or simply for the motion of leaving, he rushes back, speeding past canebrakes, propelling up bayous to his refuge. This afternoon the island glistens before him, and birds fly through streaks of sunlight. He moors his skiff to another, stepping from his bow to its stern, from one boat to another and yet another, walking his way over water. Men fishing for dinner from the dock call to him, the air full of hammering and shouts. A casual, earnest day, the men content with manual labor: repairing cabins, reinforcing sloping porches. The mosquitoes have been subdued by chilling nights, but a white sun warms the island. Daryl sprawls on the dock with the men, their banter so easy he almost misses spying Kyle and Monique exit one of the cabins. It's an image that first forms in his subconscious and then flits across the corner of his eye. Daryl raises himself with both arms and jumps abruptly to his feet.

Kyle and Monique's path leads toward the northern, wild tip of the island. He keeps his distance; they are meandering in and out of his sight and finally stop at a remote cove a half mile from the camp. Daryl steps off the path and into the forest. He leans against a smooth trunk, the mulch under his feet soft and fragrant, his vision split by arched branches. The seductive way Monique drapes herself over tangled roots as if they formed a chair while Kyle lifts himself onto a hooked branch without taking his eyes off her tells Daryl that they've been there before. They are too intent on each other to sense his presence.

"You don't love him."

Monique teases. "Why Kyle, it's you I love—always have. Just couldn't tell you 'til now," laughing sarcastically.

Daryl can hardly contain his own laughter.

But Kyle's no fool. "That's not what I meant. If I wanted your love, I wouldn't be askin' for it. I'd go out and make myself a bundle of cash." Daryl contemplates, Exactly what he's doing. "Then get my skin bleached, 'cause you don't want no Black man. Uppity white boy's more your type, fits better with what you want to be. Your bein' half white don't change the fact you're half Black. You don't love him; he's just your type."

Monique's tone turns precise. "He's what I want. Just 'cause he's my type, don't mean I can't love him. I don't allow myself to love just anybody. My man has the means and the will to get me a nice home with verandas on the first and second floors, money to roll around in, and an old family name everybody recognizes. People sniff around pedigrees like dogs smelling for a bone. I want some of that, I want to be respected. I wouldn't allow myself to love you."

There was a long silence after that. Daryl wonders why he doesn't feel used.

"The best sex I've ever had is with him."

Daryl smiles: she's looking Kyle in the eyes for that news flash.

"Yeah, well that goes, and he'll dump you, Monique, he don't need you the way you need him."

"We'll see about that," Daryl says softly.

"We'll just have to see about that," Monique spits.

Daryl could have left at that point, but he's learned from eavesdropping and gathering information for his covert endeavors, that like being half white and half Black, part of a conversation is only part of the truth. Kyle slouches in defeat. Monique must have hurt him more than she'd meant to because she feels some obligation to explain. "Kyle, my mother worked all her life to feed us, sometimes two shifts, and even then, she died in a charity ward. She never made enough no matter how hard she worked, 'cause she was never paid enough. You know what I'm talkin' about. I'm not livin' that way, and I sure as hell ain't dying that way. I wrote Beau a letter like it was from her. I need my white blood. You can't give that to me."

So, there was no proof of paternity. She had written to Beau on hearsay, maybe her mother's, maybe just gossip—a crafty choice given Beau's reputation for mixing with both races, and the fact that he wouldn't remember whether it was true or not. Very pragmatic, Daryl concludes, a fucking logic major. She had lied to him as if he were just anyone—a chump—to get his sympathy and cleave him to her. He's met Monique and her sort before: a typical local girl with a typically local ambition. And knowing that, Daryl decides, he can give her what she wants or not. He tramps back to the camp, making certain that he leaves the two of them speculating as to whom or what—man or beast—has been privy to their conversation.

# 12

## CAMP

The problem with frogs' legs, Daryl concludes, is that they jump. Night is the only time to catch frogs. Stars and moon glow over the frog capital of the world, the slimy banks of the Atchafalaya. Skinner sloshes along in the mud singing, "Jug o' rum, Jug o' rum. Bring it here, I'll give you some." Daryl's tagged along to learn the art, so instinctively repulsed by the creatures that he's stalking toe-high amphibians in hip-high rubber boots. Percy trails behind them in a pirogue, softly dipping the oars. Skinner shines a flashlight into the frogs' eyes, blinding them before they can leap. Frogs crouch facing water or submerge in it, their snouts above the surface, their eyes periscoping the night air for wispy moths. Daryl beams his flashlight at whatever's croaking, figuring the light will hit one head-on sooner or later. Once blinded, frogs are immobilized and ripe for picking. A burlap bag in the pirogue squirms, filled with sinewy flesh, attesting to Skinner's, not Daryl's, ability.

The nights have grown colder. Daryl shivers, his teeth chatter, his hands shake, even though he is muffled in a goose-down parka. He has his own system for controlling his habit, alternating his consumption of drugs and alcohol with short-lived abstinence, a task he performs, like frog hunting, with distaste. When they get back to camp, Frog King Skinner will take over. Daryl can't stomach hacking the frogs—prepping them is Skinner's job. Fastest in the world, Daryl figures, let him speed. They fry the legs in capers, pickled buds from trailing bushes. Daryl forms the capers into a little wreath of mourning sprinkled around the edge of the skillet. The frogs won't be leaping or skipping in a sprightly manner anymore, prancing in the pan each time their body fluid hits the hot oil, spitting, the rest of their bloody carcasses tossed back on the riverbank. Skinner adds salt, not too much because of the capers, then sprinkles the legs with flour so they brown evenly but still look like what they once were when it comes time to eat. If they tire of frog's legs or crayfish, perch and gar swim the lake, and duck fly overhead.

Five weeks have slipped by. The men—the chosen few and their entourages—have finished securing the camp's parameters, doing much more than Daryl finds necessary, but their number has grown as relatives and friends have gathered to work with them. They've built guard platforms to scare off inquisitive predators—not insects this round, but men and beasts—and their torches are an eerie warning in the night sky. The cabins have been repaired and spider webs swept out of every corner. Fires in the central kitchen burn into the night, heating food. There is one simple overnight rule: bring your own bedroll. Cane Island has become not only a haven for the precious few involved in Daryl's business, but for their assistants and supplicants, enablers and abettors, and applauders and hangers-on. According to Daryl, discretion's gone to hell in a hand basket. Never mind that they're running a legitimate trapping business; selling frogs and crawfish is a convenient ruse, but this, even with Daryl's love of flamboyance, is too much. The whole countryside must be aware of the missing throng.

Who are these men who arrive as adjuncts to his men? They are those who have been mislaid: fourth son, youngest of seven brothers, husband of the third daughter, one of five brothers-in-law, ex-husbands, all gamblers with nothing to lose by crashing on the shore of Daryl's island. They camp in makeshift tents, shack up in the cabins, and dine out of the same pots. Each man belongs to a unit; each unit has a chief, now flush with cash, a private army of sorts.

Daryl has commandeered one cabin for himself and Monique, and Michael sleeps in the main cabin, which doubles as an office. He has found something he loves doing: counting money. Kyle bunks with him, guarding his share, propped on the front porch maintaining his post. The men look to Kyle before they look to anyone else. Money flows in spurts, and they've settled into their roles. Overall vision and ultimate expansion are Daryl's, the mastermind who stays remote and entertaining. Michael runs the daily operation: accounts to be paid, collateral to be redeemed, and the subsequent quantities to be dispensed, depending on previous sales records. Kyle, when he's not off on his own business, functions as liaison to the men, keeping them in order. Skinner and Percy oversee cooking, sleeping arrangements, and food deliveries. And Monique? Monique struts about the camp: a high-stepping, swaybacked, bust-

busting, ripe-butt-sticking-out strut.

She's the Queen of Cane Island, who makes certain that all the men want her before she wraps herself around Daryl, her trophy. She clings to him in a desperate tug, Daryl pulling away, Monique insisting, her pelvis pressed against his crotch, her tongue sliding up his neck. She doesn't wait to be alone with him, and he's unsure of how far she would go right there on the stilted porch and in full view, if he were to accommodate her persistent fondling. Sometimes it arouses him, his power over her, the performance, the grunts from the peanut gallery, especially his watching Kyle—who tries not to look and more often than not fails—but sooner than later Daryl gets disgusted with her groping. It's not his desire Monique wants, it's the men's desire to be in his place and have his prerogatives. Her desire is contingent upon this public display, their desire for her, not hers for him. That's where she gets her kicks. He's almost ready to give her over to Kyle, but Kyle seems sick of it, too.

Daryl guides Monique inside his cabin. He unbuttons her blouse; she's quiet and accommodating. Reckons she owes it to me, Daryl observes, as he pushes her down on the bed, towering over her in disdain. "If you can't behave yourself, leave here." He stops at the threshold, a soft wind teasing the branches outside, before slamming the door hard as he exits, so everyone can hear that he doesn't want her. He assumes that she'll stay behind, shamed by his indifference, but she follows him out to the porch, her shirt open to expose nut-colored breasts, her hands on swaying hips, and scans the crew, who stare in appreciation. She tosses Daryl a look: *Hundreds do want me, not just the ones in this dump.* He has to smile, his eyes full of her, and she telepaths a message straight into him: *Only they can't have me, I'm doin' the picking, and I pick you.* Monique's made him fall for her all over again.

The men are distracted; Noland's making an entrance, steering his speedboat into the cove, gunning his motor like he's Evil Knievel, but his boat's not cooperating, accelerating, then coughing its way to the island. Sunning by the pier, they laugh with anticipation as to just how Noland's going to make a fool of himself. Daryl mounts the stairs to their office; Noland's got to dock, walk through the men, then climb up the stairs to him. Michael's counting money, separating it into piles.

"Happy?" Daryl asks.

"I think it's happening, I mean, I think it's working."

Just the cash, that's all he needs, he has no idea where I'm taking us, Daryl thinks.

"Unfuckingbelievable."

"Don't get too delirious, might have to give you mouth to mouth." Daryl looks over his shoulder to check Noland's progress; commotion and riotous laughter as Noland tries to step onto the dock. The men are rocking his boat.

"Looks like Noland found us."

Michael bags the money. Good, Daryl thinks, fact he wants to hide it means he won't interfere with my next move. "What's our arrangement with Noland again?"

It's rote by now. "We pay him twenty percent."

"So let's pay the sheriff ten percent, direct."

Noland enters; his trousers are soaked from the knees down.

"Well, look what we got here."

Noland sputters, furious, "Where you be at, what's goin' on?"

Daryl's playing host. "Our little distribution center, Noland, our territory and private property, but don't wait for an invite, make yourself at home."

"You got my field labor out here. I need them."

"They don't get paid enough. Besides, they're not yours. Which brings me to you.  Noland, what are we paying you for?"

Michael shoots a patronizing reminder, "Noland set us up, Daryl. We owe him."

But Daryl's not talking to Michael. "Seems to me, the good ol' boy network suffers from too much nepotism, all that revenue being siphoned off, encourages inbreeding. Wouldn't you say, Noland?"

A fool, yes, a fish, no, Noland won't rise to the bait.

Daryl doesn't need him. He mimics Noland's spindly legs and elastic pelvis perfectly. "Why is that, Daryl?" Daryl shifts from impersonating Noland back to himself. "Have nothing to do but sit around and fuck each other, Noland."

Noland's about to implode, but Kyle's closing in behind him.

"Cut it, Daryl." That's from Michael.

Daryl ignores him. "Noland, you have the same access to that boat captain, the one who calls himself Arevan, as we do. You are now free to do whatever you like with your connection."

Noland turns to Michael, "What're you doing with him?"

Michael's waiting for the other shoe to drop.

Daryl's cue, "Noland, how long you been taking a cut from Michael's sales?"

Noland squawks at Michael, "I don't take a cut—I sell to you!"

But there's no escaping Daryl. "No you don't, Arevan does. You've been taking a cut for a simple introduction, something other people do just to be polite."

Noland truly believes Daryl doesn't understand. "Tell the fuck—"

Confrontations and Michael don't mix. "Forget it, he's wired, it's not happening."

Men crowd the porch.

"Let me put it this way, No-land. What you buy is yours to keep, and you don't have to split it with Michael and me anymore." Daryl hands Noland a bundle of cash, "Severance, you're fired."

Noland clutches the cash, his fingers turning yellow. He screams to the men as if he's got friends on the porch to back him up. "Squatting in a colored cabin, tellin' me what to do?" Then he turns to Michael. "Set him straight!" and having spewed saliva everywhere, he storms down the stairs, spindly white arms waving like flags.

The men chant after him, "No-land, No-land, No-land!"

Michael and Daryl watch from the door. Night's coming, and the last light bounces off the skiffs; laughter rises as Noland pushes through the men on his way to the dock.

"Get that candy ass on back to the fields."

"Cut it yourself."

There's a peace here Daryl's never known before.

Noland, almost to the dock and in sight of his transportation, gets cocky, yelling up to Daryl, "You think you got something here, you got nothing: a nigra's island, a nigra army, and a nigra fuck. You're nothing. A nobody."

Why isn't he afraid, hurling insults surrounded as he is? Daryl wonders. Maybe it's our laughter, low and easy, that's fooling him, or maybe he figures we have better things to do than get stuck with Murder One. At the moment Daryl can't think of what, but he's feeling too satisfied to move. Or perhaps it's that Noland believes he's still on the Monroe plantation and has the imprimatur of white protection, because that's how he's acting. Skinner pulls the line mooring Noland's boat up to the dock. His pose mimics the liveried lanterns placed in front of ostentatious homes, his smile a grimace of welcome, or in this case farewell. He dangles the rope. "Here you are, sir."

Noland screeches "Get your hands off my boat."

Skinner drops the line, shoves the boat with his toe, not so anyone would notice, and holds that grin. Skinner has style: substance can always hit the high note, but style carries it off. Noland steps onto thin air, arms pinwheeling, legs flopping like Raggedy Andy. On the way down he hits the cartilage that holds up his nose on the boat rail before he slips into the lake. A tumultuous mess surfacing to applause and more laughter, Noland's all snot and blood. The men pull him out and toss him into his speedboat, shoving it toward St. Martinville. Only a fool like Noland could be blind to the hate seething beneath the eyes of the disinherited. That anger's patient, bloodlust, not envy, bides its time until the time is right. Daryl senses what he cannot see. Nostrils flare, tongues taste salt—just like before a kill.

But tonight, the men feast in celebration of the returns on the first shipment.  They've sold the last of it, not in record time, but there will be time enough for that. The light sinks into the lake. Without the sun, the air is sharp with cold. They start more fires for warmth, light more torches to cut the darkness. The rains are coming, the real ones.  Not the wild spurts that threatened the harvest, but full-blown, endless months of rain.  The lake steams: waters warmed by the sun condense in cool air and turn to mist. Fog heavy with cold settles in their midst. Men huddle, speaking in soft hazy murmurs around their fires. Someone's brought reefers. Monique draws the weed's smoke between her lips. Daryl pulls her mouth to his; smoke seeps from her breath and fills his lungs. Daryl's skin is damp but he feels no cold. He lies suspended, the air magnetic. He gets high to flee, but in Monique's arms, her lap his pillow and his head cushioned in sweet flesh, he feels faint. Monique kisses his lips; he's on solid ground yet the sky reels, as in vertigo. Night sounds meander, the only movement is the lilt of arms and feet, the silent sifting of smoke. Food is passed from hand to hand. Fingers, Monique's, probe a bowl to pick crayfish, pungent flesh for his lips. Grasping, his mouth open, he sucks the flesh from her fingers, the morsels slippery with oil. Food dissolves in his mouth. Juices drip down his chin. Monique wipes his face with her skirt. Daryl almost cries out; I am afraid to love.

He's ascribed his need for her to lust, certain it will pass. But in their sex, speaking in moans and cries, thrashing like fish in air, there's a desperate communication. He can't let go of her.

The clapping starts first, soft palms form a languid percussion, the drums follow, ardent beat from someplace else, and the spoons, staccato, almost lyrical, lead the washboard, a syncopated form of harmony that reminds someone to blow into a harmonica, its music winding through the camp. The insects still to listen. A fieldworker dances to the stars, a slow methodical arch. Daryl lies half on Monique's lap and half on the earth, his head thrown back as if in sleep. Michael's foot, garbed in muddy cowhide, falls next to Daryl's ear. He sniffs Michael's scent through the seams. Michael's hands wrap around Daryl's biceps and pull him up. Daryl tries to stand, his head spins. The cedar torches smoke. The sky has cleared; stars pile up in a center-less night. It's impossible for Daryl to walk without swaying, but Michael's arm clenches his ribs, Michael's right leg supports his left leg. They dance this way, Michael's blood coursing, heating Daryl's movements—until Michael pushes him away.

Circling the camp in a night cold with stars, a heron glides above the beating drums. The joy must be in riding the winds, to float skimming air. Far below its wingspan, Michael lifts his toes, bends his knees and curves his hands to apex at his crown like antlers. It's not until he sniffs the air poised to flee that Daryl sees him as a deer. They learned this dance from Beau. The clapping becomes more insistent. The hunted scents the hunter. Daryl inhales and with each subsequent breath comes lucidity. He dances to stalk, circling Michael's would-be flight. The more fretful Michael's movements become, the slower, more precise are Daryl's, until he has Michael trapped.

Noland has fled to the houseboat to plead for help, as if his predicament is Arevan's problem. He waits there, shaking with cold, his nose broken, swollen and deformed. Damage begs for damage. The strong prey on the weak. Arevan does his own killing when crossed, expects no mercy and gives none in return. His strength lies in understanding and respecting the natural order of things. In his panic, Noland has forgotten that his problem is his own to resolve; and if he sinks, he sinks alone.

Arevan leaves Noland pleading for mercy. First, Noland's hands are tied behind his back. Then he is tossed, a human punching bag, between Arevan and Jorge. Fists hit ripe, juicy flesh: Noland is sickeningly malleable. When he slumps half-dead, Arevan whispers, "Enough." Jorge stops mid-punch and withdraws. Arevan whispers into Noland's ear, "We accepted the Monroe boy on your word."

Noland gargles through his blood, "I know his family."

"Everyone knows his family." Arevan wipes the blood from Noland's mouth. "What do you want Noland, more than anything?"

Noland rasps, "For you to get your fucking hands off me."

"Ask me for something else."

Noland's ability to speak fails him.

"Remember hell?"

This raises Noland, as if through a strainer. "For everything to go back the way it was. That's all I want."

"Then fix it, return it to the way it was." And, just before Noland passes out, "Remember Noland, fear makes men sway."


Daryl groans, hugging his chest. The air is cold, and his muscles shiver and convulse, even with Monique twined around his back for warmth. He opens his eyes but keeps his breathing shallow. She curls closer and he lies still, willing her to sleep. When her breath on his neck slows, he disengages from her hold. He feels like the day after a stag party, his insides bloated and raw. Rising from the ground becomes an unimaginable effort, his head throbbing so that it takes him a full minute to unbend and stand. The view doesn't help—a squalid camp. Men are sprawled about the yard in unsanitary clumps like the dead after a battle. Daryl heads for Michael's cabin; he inadvertently kicks a leg as he tries to maneuver a path through the sleepers. No one wakes. Daryl closes his eyes. The sun's a searchlight gleaming through his eyelids, luminous through his veins, rust colored. Michael's cabin is only a few staggering steps away. They keep the Alka-Seltzer in the cash box along with the Maalox and the paregoric.

The cabin doesn't smell right; the air is not stuffy with sleep or noisy with snores. He opens an interior door and sees Michael's empty cot, no pile of dirty clothes and no knapsack. When he opens the cash box three bundles are intact: Kyle's, Skinner's, and his own, but Michael's is missing. Clarity turns him sober. He stands on the porch whistling in agony. The dogs are gone. He scans the shore to find a gaping hole among the boats where Michael's skiff was moored. All Daryl can think is that he's not coming back. The sun, rising, shimmers off the lake. Currents rush toward the river and the anxious tow of the sea. The coming rains will swell the bayou and partly flood the island. Daryl's trial run has been a haphazard success, but the men have been too brazen and uncontrollable. Many are leaving today. Daryl and Michael have decided to make operations small for the winter, like a private hunting camp, so they can reorganize, leaving only Kyle, Percy, Skinner, and a small cadre accountable to them.

Now what? Daryl wonders. Michael's left him. He stares at the dock in disbelief, willing him back. Waves slap against the boats lying along the shore, half on land, half in water. His thoughts spin. The one he was counting on has slipped away, and he can't be sure whose side Michael has chosen. Daryl mistook Michael's passive acceptance of his decisions as a sign of allegiance. But the natural order of things had been established long before his return, and Michael clings to habit. He's not imaginative enough to see things otherwise. Daryl had thought that given the opportunity, Michael would want to flee from the confines of subsistence dealing—if Daryl led him to it. Instead, it's Michael leaving him—Daryl seethes—back to his suffocating village, his nothing home, and his hick cohorts.

# 13

# ERATH

The dogs smell him first, jumping from the couches to whine at the back door, their noses pressed into the screen: eggs, bacon, brewing coffee. Michael hesitates, one foot on the porch, but Mae's at the door raising the latch, dogs rushing past her legs, her arms open wide in welcome. Short and stocky, Mae is deceptively well proportioned until she's hugged, then the small waist and high round breasts make their full impression. Her downy mouth brushes Michael's cheek. He's known her almost all his life. After his grandparents died, whenever Beau would return, Mae would move in with the two men. Beau was all she talked about, until her constancy made him in her eyes—if not his own—*his*. Beau didn't give it much thought, but he let her love him. He'd come back, the house dowdy with Michael's bachelordom, and in a matter of days Mae would show up— uncalled for—and air the sheets, Pine-Sol every room, wax the floors, and do the shopping, the cooking, and Beau's bidding. Circling his bed in deference, conceding everything, to lie untouched by his side, or square and shivering under his weight. When Beau left to tour, or to carouse, or just to leave, she would wait a few days, dusting the table with her fingers, cooking for Michael and herself, and then pack her overnight case, fold whatever didn't fit into a plastic garbage bag, load her rickety car, and retreat down the long drive to disappear, giving Michael back his solitude. All this was familiar to Michael. He hesitated because he thought things had changed, that he would have his father all to himself today, there at the farmhouse, waiting for him. But Mae had never gotten between the two of them and even now she withdraws, slipping into the back room as he enters.

Famished, Michael heads for the kitchen. Beau watches from his place at the table. Nothing's left to eat; greasy pans are stacked in the sink, but coffee percolates on the stove.

"From what I hear, you ain't shackin' up with anybody."

Michael searches the cabinets. "You askin' where I've been?"

"Ain't on the road..."

Michael retrieves a miniature box of Cheerios from an assorted pack, grabs a carton of milk from the counter, and sits by Beau. He cuts the box's cardboard perforations, leak proof with wax paper, engineering it into an instant bowl, and splashes milk into the cereal—Cheerios bob in bantam waves. As if it were an afterthought, Michael pulls a bundle of cash from his back pocket and shoves the money toward his father's plate.

"This is for you." He rises to look for a spoon, turning his back on Beau as if it doesn't matter.

Beau's in the same position of condescension, the cash untouched, when Michael sits back down. He straddles the chair, pretending to concentrate on the tiny life preservers in milky sea.

"I got it for you."

"I don't want it."

Michael glances at Beau, a sidelong, slow-to-comprehend, furtive glance.

One truculent sweep of Beau's arm sends the cash fanning across the table; twenty-dollar bills flutter to the floor. "Think you came back here to some blathering fool. Your old man drool, yet? You see saliva drippin' from my lips?"

Michael's hands stroke the oilcloth, gathering his offering, his efforts attenuated by his distress. "Beau, take it," leaning over, picking up stranded bills. "I did this for you."

"For me!" Beau uncoils like a snake, slapping the money from Michael's hands, slapping his palms across Michael's face.

Michael raises his arms, shielding himself. "Stop!"

Beau stops to catch his breath. Michael straightens his chair, his shirt.

Beau leans into Michael. "You've been selling coke to Black people, friends of mine, at clubs I've been playing at. Using *me* to sell drugs to people who can hardly make ends meet."

Beau's eyes are mining his face. Michael deflects, "It's got nothin' to do with you."

"It has everything to do with me. I did it with friends, to cover expenses. Getting high's a personal matter, Michael. You're selling drugs to people you don't know. You've made it into a business."

Michael's ears flare red. "Yeah? And what was I supposed

to do? You make next to nothing. What the hell you think we've been livin' on? Where the fuck've you been?"

Beau lifts his hands as if to stop Michael's anger and backs away. "Don't do this for me." And finally, "You call Daryl back, get him involved in this?"

Michael says nothing; his father's assumption hurts the most.

Beau persists. "He'll take the fall with you."

Michael snorts, "I can take care of Daryl."

"And who's going to care for you?"

"I'm not stupid and I'm not naive; I make payoffs."

"Like me, you mean, not stupid like me."

Exactly.

"You're nothing better than a thief. Get out of my house."

Michael's incredulous. "It's my house!"

Mae reenters: she was eavesdropping. "Beau, everyone thought you knew. I thought you knew."

Beau turns on her. "You thought I *knew*?" and spits at Michael—"You shame me, both of you, but you most of all—" before marching out of the house.

Michael says, "Mae, I did do it for him."

"Honey, he never asked you to."

"Why do you stay with him?" As if she's the only fool. "Why don't you leave?"

Mae smooths her skirt, searching the floor for an answer, helpless with concern. "You don't understand."

"What don't I understand?"

They hear Beau start his car, then drive away.

Michael says, "I can help you Mae, you need money."

"No, darlin', no. It's not that." She's reaching for the right words, finding none. "You've got to find another way to live."

"What? What could I do that would be enough for him? He doesn't care what I do. He doesn't love us, Mae, he doesn't even see us."

"He cares, Michael. He's afraid."

"Afraid of what?"

"He's afraid of losing you. He runs because he's in pain. He runs away to get the losing of you over with." And, thinking of her own dilemma. "How could we leave him? What would he have left?"

# 14

# MORGAN CITY

Daryl slips into his car, his mind is racing in place, his thoughts are flip-flopping, piling up one on top of other: Monique was awake, she watched Michael go. Monique *and* Michael are against him. Monique wants Michael out of the picture, so she can have Daryl all to herself. Either way she's dangerous, interfering with his plans. And Kyle? Kyle's got his own agenda. Always keep your enemies close by your side so you can watch them. Edgy distinction between friends and foes—and between lovers, betrayal's implicit. Monique doesn't love me, Daryl concludes, she hates white men. Why shouldn't she, invisible and nonexistent as she is to her own daddy—whomever that is. Love lives just around the corner from hate.

He speeds over an empty county highway down the center of the two-lane road. Daryl has a goal, but what it is eludes him. Water drifts over marshland, and he's headed south to Morgan City and its lattice coast. He can't stop the rant in his head, contorting his conclusion into fact: Morgan City, where Noland has all those connections on his father's rigs, working the old man like a harmonica; awfully smart, Daryl concedes, for somebody so dumb. But Daryl's true rage is bent upon Michael: Michael never had any respect for Noland's squirrely existence before, but then Noland stayed in the Parish and languished like the rest of them, while Daryl left them behind for a pricey big-city school.

Daryl figures he's at a disadvantage in many respects. For instance, Daryl's guessing, Noland and Michael could be with Arevan, and here he is driving into a trap. His objective is to intercept the damage with his presence, and through his charm and reassurance, usurp Noland's minor position. Although the logical part of him is thinking that Noland and Michael haven't done anything—they're just pacing and contorting up in St. Martinville, or Erath, or huddled into a booth at Leroy's trying to figure out the next step, leaving him to clear the way for Arevan's greed. That's where he'd headed, toward Arevan's territory.

Daryl turns his attention to the two-block villages he's speeding through and vows he'll never end up in one. Each hamlet supports a rice mill at one end and a Mobil gas station at its other, the winged horse an emblem of greeting or farewell. Between the two, depending upon each village, are a string of low-rise stores, abandoned or not, painted in pastel shades of comfort or left to weather, impoverished or substantial—dry goods stores, oyster houses, and bars— where, parallel to their back doors, a railroad line links the rice mills. Daryl zooms through at least two or three Rice Capitals of the World and curses. Thirty-mile-an-hour speed zone so it'll take longer, make the town seem bigger. And then his mind flips again: Monique knew Michael was leaving, he's sure of it.

Monique had lifted her head to see the men scattered like stones and Michael striding above them, picking his way through bundled sleepers, his knapsack slung over his shoulder. She watched his progress, saw him trip, then catch himself, load his skiff, push it from the dock. At first, he rowed the boat away from the island. When he softly turned the motor; no one else heard. His boat floated past the far shore, the first pink rays of the sun glistening over a shimmering lake.

Daryl's car swats by roadside chicken stands and one-room music clubs. At the Blue Goose he thinks, That's me, a fool. Passing a burnt-out hulk called the Blue Moon, he thinks, Once in a blue moon you'd think maybe you could trust somebody. Then, ten miles later, at the Blue Angel, She does love me and I'm paranoid. He's sliding through stop signs, one per town, idling at a crossroad with its traffic light blinking red in the Frog, Alligator, Crawfish, or Nutria Capital until he arrives at a place he believes is the capital of all that swims or crawls and decides to stop for lunch, to go, because he's in a rush. A sign displays the menu: "Oysters, fresh garfish, catfish, turtle, fresh goo, live crabs. Come on in."

He's heading south toward the Gulf, racing past flat marshland. He mutters to himself, "Maybe she just didn't care if Michael left, because she didn't need him anymore." Truth is, he concludes, Monique *doesn't* need Michael anymore, but I do.

At the outskirts of Morgan City, he slams on the brakes;

ahead lies what looks like a necropolis. Oil refineries, a multitude of blackened towers with grilled pinnacles and blinking lights that warn off the small planes. There is not a soul in sight. Daryl pulls over for a substantial hit, calculating that he can't get arrested in a necropolis because he's not dead yet. And then the thought passes before him: Jesus, what if I am in one of those stories where my life is about to sweep by, and this is purgatory? Daryl checks the horizon, dotted with little Eiffel Towers as far as his eye can see. No figures flit between the electrical lines, no Dante, no Robert Johnson…. Calmer, he slides into first gear. The coast is a mile away, and beyond the coast, the barrier islands and the rigs.

Helicopters fly riggers to and from the farthest oil platforms in the Gulf of Mexico while motorboats bus the men who work on rigs closer to the coast. Daryl's tried to imagine that life. Two weeks off to be with family, then two weeks on in seventy-mile-an-hour winds and piercing rain in the winter, grueling sun in summer, with the men clinging to cables, the ocean ripping at the platform, fitted pipes creaking at the joints. The noise a blare of chaos day and night, night's uncreated darkness blending with the rig's lights. Men are fragile as light if a rig blows, the ocean sprouting fire. Escape, roast or drown.

Arevan busses men burdened with loneliness and worry. Daryl knows this for a fact, because while Arevan looks as if he could captain a fishing trawler, he doesn't smell it, and Daryl's seen the kind of motorboats Arevan and Noland use to ferry men back and forth from rigs to shore. Radar on the helm aids navigation through the fog, among other things. Daryl has imagined it all: Arevan watches each shipment arrive on his boat with one of the riggers but does not lay hands on it. It's left under a seat when the carrier departs. Arevan simply takes this same boat up some inland slough, then a 30-minute ride to rendezvous with Noland, and then Michael comes in to the picture.

Daryl drives to the busiest wharf. Why draw attention by picking somewhere obscure? It's best to get lost in a crowd. He asks the dock master what's coming in or out from the Vermilion Platforms and the man tells him he's got five minutes. That's where most of the pins were on the map in the library, ruby red for Vermilion Bay. So Daryl's not surprised when, standing on the edge of a dock, overlooking a choppy sea, he sees Arevan's boat ripping toward the wharf, a thin line of white foam advancing to greet him. The riggers disembark and file past him, ragged and exhausted. Arevan docks the boat there, the last to leave. He hesitates briefly when he spots Daryl, then strolls by without acknowledging him. He has the same dark, moody eyes, the same laughing grimace that Daryl remembers from the houseboat. He can't tell if Noland's talked to Arevan yet or not. He reckons not, ship to shore being a wide-open channel.

Daryl falls in step with Arevan. "Hey!" striding beside him.

Arevan ignores him and keeps walking.

Daryl sprints ahead to turn and stand in front of Arevan,

stopping him, and concentrates on just one of his eyes.

His gaze tips Arevan off balance. "I don't know you."

Daryl insists. "Houseboat, Coulee Channel."

Arevan's tone carries a threat. "I said: I don't know you."

He's right, he doesn't, but they've met. Daryl extends his hand. "Daryl Monroe, St. Martinville. You work for my father." Daryl doesn't think he does, but he's testing.

"I work for nobody."

"Good. Because I have a proposal, between us."

Arevan retreats, back to the privacy of his slip where he pretends to be checking the lines that secure his boat. He starts to retie one as Daryl hunkers down next to him.

"A partnership. We access the platforms through your associates, and I supply all the labor for distribution."

"I give you my associates, you give me yours?"

"Exactly, fifty-fifty."

"I don't want a partner." Arevan moves to the next line.

Daryl follows him. "My father owns those rigs. You pay him a cut for using his facilities?" This isn't a threat, just a simple fact coupled with a legitimate query.

Arevan shifts his weight as if he were about to rise and throttle him. "You work for your daddy?"

"If I did, you'd already be workin' with us. Drop Noland, deal directly with me."

"What the fuck, I don't give a damn about Noland, take the whole parish."

Daryl laughs. "I can triple your business."

"But double my profits." Arevan ties the next sailor's

knot as if he were strangling Daryl with it.

Daryl smiles, the discrepancy's better than what he's got now.

"Then I get rid of Jorge, huh? Dumb wetback, who gives a fuck? Right?"

Daryl's irritated. "I could care less what you do with Jorge the motherfucker."

Arevan mimics him. "Could care less," relishing his little joke. "And Michael?"

Bingo, he sees Daryl's doubt, what he's been looking for—the reason for Michael's absence.

"Michael's with me."

"Michael's with you." Arevan looks around, mocking Daryl. "So where is he?"

"He had other business to attend to."

"I see. So once you have my people dropping to your people on your daddy's rigs, I'll be the one who looks expendable to you. And Michael." Arevan sneers. "Or maybe you look expendable to me and Michael?"

Daryl steps back into the twilight. "Think about it. I'll be back, but not for a while. See what Noland can afford to buy without us."

Walking to the parking lot, the light dimming, the clouds dark gray in a pale sky, Daryl soothes himself: Arevan was fishing. Daryl started his trip haunted by Michael's absence and ends it relieved at his absence. By the time he's reached his car, the problem seems simple: If things don't go his way, he'll starve them out.

Starve them out. Daryl likes the sound of it. Perhaps he'll take a trip in the meantime, go back to New Orleans where, if he has no friends left, a few of his old crowd might be willing to float him some cash for an ample return. Something Daryl wants to have at his fingertips when Arevan gets hungry enough.

Arevan is not as hungry as Daryl would like to believe. He manifests himself into the captain of a ferryboat or a shrimp trawler, transforms from a taciturn good ol' boy into a cold-blooded killer, at will. Arevan disguises himself by being exactly who he is, a local. Arevan is cunning, he'll only intervene when Noland fails; until then, he can wait.

# 15

# The Storm

A storm followed Daryl up the coast, hounding his fears. The car radio warned drivers of flooded roads to come, pilots of dangerous winds, captains of unpredictable currents. He sought refuge in his father's library, relieved to postpone whatever awaited him on Cane Island. The house was dark and silent, an oasis from the wild clatter squalling toward the parish.

If you were to beseech Daryl with a fearful, What have you done? he would respond with, Rebuilt an outpost, fired a jerk, inadvertently alienated Michael, posited a query or two, and forced a proposal of sorts to Arevan. But what's seen and heard is shadowed by what's imagined, and what's imagined is equal parts terror and desire. What has Daryl done? He's set hearsay loose, his words and deeds scattering like straw in the wind.

Gusts pass through the open windows. Daryl can't find *Metamorphoses*; it's not on the shelf where he left it. He settles on a picture book, but he's unable to concentrate, flipping by lush painted surfaces flattened by the printer's ink, pages falling in capricious display, a panoply of nineteenth-century vision, revolutions in surface, perspective and history, until he comes to a painting, deceptive in its simplicity since its subjects—a Mulatto girl and a blue heron, could never have been in such close proximity before their joining on the canvas. The girl bears Monique's profile;

she is a blueprint for his lover's face. Clearly at one time she occupied the whole painting, its source of inspiration and focus. Her eyes, exotic with kohl, contemplate the strange world before her—Daryl's world. She is unaware of her companion; they occupy the same space but not the same plane. The heron floats beside her, an afterthought in transcendent blue painted to keep the bird suspended and stationary by her side. Her concentrated attempt to ignore the heron, which, like all wading birds becomes darker and more sumptuous when courting, turns its presence into a lurid intrusion. Daryl wants the bird to caress her cheek, lift its indigo wings, and stroke her hair. He licks the plumage, its feathers painted like cake frosting, but the reproduction's ink is bitter, not sweet.

What could never have existed exists now in his mind, and he bursts with longing for their union, his dark lover and the gray-blue bird, for her teeth to sink into its neck, thirsting with lust. Wings beat her breasts; beak and claws streak her soft flesh as the bird plunges and plunges. Monique gasps in awe and horror. Her arms turn to wings, her breasts, pressing against the bird's chest, puff with feathers, plumage grows from her belly, and her cries turn to caws. What's imagined is equal parts terror and desire. A diorama of separate worlds, theirs and his, like a coast that curves from placid sands into the wild lure of the sea, the hypnotic pull of its waters, one step from this dimension into the undertow of another plane. He is stunned and muted by this beauty that does not recognize his existence.

The sky snaps, swelled by heat and cold, a crash that could wake the dead. A thin crack of lightning illuminates the dark clouds, and sheaths of rain, waterspouts, drown all other sounds. The library's French doors are open to the elements, silk curtains stretch and flap. A vase overturns, and flowers and water splatter the carpet. Daryl watches, hypnotized. Rain dapples the room; a lamp falls. His father, unaware of Daryl's presence, is walking down the hallway toward the library, coming to close the doors. Daryl hears his footsteps. The library is his sanctuary, his father's condescension his internment. He moves with such effort, as if he's returning from a distant place, and escapes into the storm just as Joseph enters the room. Unlatched, a door bangs. Joseph looks as if he's seen a ghost, standing at the threshold, pelted by rain and leaves, he calls out, "Is that you? Please God, don't leave me."

His plea is lost to the tempest, which is the only justification Joseph has for allowing himself this luxury, wailing for his wife. The night conceals Daryl, and a callused oak buffers him against the rain. Fitful, he turns from his father's agony. Clouds mass and roll, rain falls in sheets to pound and flood the earth. Birds who have not found refuge ride on gusts of wind, pale flashes in the lightning, dusky black in the night. When Daryl turns back the doors are closed, and the windows are shut. Through a crack in streaming water, he sees that Joseph has withdrawn to sit by the fireplace, slumped in defeat. They are both crying. Daryl was the one who left, and in leaving, let her go.

He spent the rest of the night dozing fitfully in his car, its red exterior a cocoon. The black rain pounding its roof, pouring down its windows, subsided before dawn. Awakening to a gray mist, his father's house looming behind him, Daryl relieved himself on the driveway in full view of its windows and coughed the sleep from his bones.

When he reaches Cane Island after maneuvering his boat through the damp cold, his enclave of shacks on the hill looks hollow and shabby. No activity reveals its inhabitants. He docks, the shoreline is empty and bleak. Rain drips from the trees, trampled grasses clot the path as he climbs up the incline. Cane Island smells foul, its mud and shacks have been abandoned by most of the men. The remaining skiffs have been brought up to the cabins and turned upside down by the kitchen. Daryl's core group is asleep, or so he assumes. Kyle's boat is propped against a cabin wall, but Michael's skiff is still missing. Whether Monique is here or not, innocent or complicit, with him or against him, are all possibilities he has yet to parse out. When Daryl gets to his cabin, he hears Kyle speaking with her inside. Their voices, sultry and languid, ripple like laughter. He barges in as they're mid-sentence.

It hangs unfinished, Kyle's mouth open, Monique in bed, barely dressed. Kyle is seated beside her, fully clothed, Daryl notes, but, hell, all he'd have to do is zip it up.

"Kyle, you were saying?" Daryl asks.

It's a big question; both Kyle and Monique are silent as they adjust, Kyle looking at Monique for guidance. There is a rapport between them that Daryl will never like. Her eyes ask Kyle to leave, and he understands, rising from the bed.

"What Monique confides in me is private. And what y'all discuss ain't none of my business." He holds Daryl's gaze and then passes out the door before Monique can catch her breath.

"Sleep well?" Daryl asks.

"You left me here, lying half-naked with a whole pack of men!"

Daryl's impressed, humping all night and she turns it around as if it were his fault she's screwing somebody else. "So pack, we're leaving."

Monique doesn't budge. Daryl thinks that they could be up to anything. He could choke the life from her, one hand around her neck, but when he gets close enough, his thumb stroking her windpipe, her spices flare up his nostrils and the longing for her almost chokes him.

"You want to stay here without me?"

Monique takes her time telling him, "I don't want to do anything without you."

Daryl needs another several days, eardrums pounding, to finally hear her. What he manages to say in the meantime, "You're mine, or the deal's off" sounds like a trade agreement.

Monique's pragmatic. "If we leave, what happens then?"

Seems like hedging to Daryl. "What happens to who?"

Monique flinches. "The others. The men."

"They'll wait. Maybe Kyle can take care of them, too."

Monique looks away in anger.

All this banter, Daryl thinks, but what I'm really doing is begging. "I want to know that nobody else touches you. That's what I want."

Monique hesitates, her eyes bound around the room, around him.

And he understands; she's afraid he doesn't mean it. He opens his arms.

"You want me or not?"

She's wrapped around him, and he feels like a rock, crushing her to his chest like foam, his body remolding to fit the contours of her form, his breath washing over her.

She whispers into his ear, "Nobody else, nobody else, ever."

After they've melted and molted over the floor, the bed, the piles of clothes, and sent everything on the bed stand tumbling over, things feel stable enough for Daryl to convince them both that his prevarication's the truth.

"We got to go to New Orleans so y'all can meet my partner, he's nervous about the money."

"I thought Michael and I were your partners?"

Her naïveté makes him laugh, its sincerity a balm. "Honey, I got partners everywhere I go, how I stay in business."

"Are we all the same split, fifty-fifty?"

Adding and subtracting already: what's hers, what's his, back to square one, forget love. Daryl hides his anger and leverages his offer with a bribe. "We'll make it into a vacation: restaurants, parties, new clothes."

Monique curls into his chest to hide, and he cradles her trying to figure what this is; he smells fear. She's hardly breathing.

"You ever been anywhere else before?"

"No, never."

No. Never. Never loved anyone else like him before either, so how the hell would she know? And he'd like to crush her for good, anger welling up, feeling exposed.

"Where's Michael?"

Monique senses danger: it can make even the truth shaky. "He went back to his daddy, to give him all his money, *cher*, what he always does."

Daryl's uncertainty falls away. Michael went back to Beau, and when he's done lapping up whatever warmth Beau will make available to him, Michael will come back to him. The old familiar past stretches before him like a searchlight. What the hell, Daryl reflects, everything's just fucking what it always was.

Except that the obvious had eluded him. While his mind was trotting the four directions, spinning nowhere, Michael had been walking the straight and narrow path toward home. No betrayal, no subterfuge, no alliance other than the one he's always pursued. No matter what Beau did, or didn't do, to deserve such devotion. Daryl winces: what he has to fear most from Michael is his loyalty. Daryl decides that not only does he have to quell Michael's anxiety over the little scene with Noland, but he also has to keep him unaware of his meeting with Arevan. He'll take Michael to New Orleans. Until Arevan, left with Noland's limitless inability, is ready to concede.

# 16

## El Dorado

Leroy has called the entire crowd to the main door of his bar. Its windows can't hold their curiosity, so they pour into the parking lot, cursing merciless fate to have been born to this. Two men whom they have always addressed with assurance are now causing envy and dismay, a betrayal tantamount to treason. Matthew has made it his business to sound the alarm: Percy and Skinner have bought themselves a gold Cadillac Eldorado convertible—secondhand, but still; it's parked down the street in front of the General Store. The top is down and they're filling the backseat and the trunk with their purchases: a Sony television, fans, a clock radio, a stereo and speakers with quadraphonic sound, a vacuum cleaner, and in a trailer off the car's bumper, a Frigidaire. It seems they've bought everything in the store except the freezer cases, the cash register, and the cashier.

Percy and Skinner ignore their audience, disgruntled white men stamping in the lot down the road, hands deep in pockets fashioned by Levi Strauss, fingering dirty bills to reckon their worth—the number of beers, or gas for the car, or rice and beans for dinner—until the convertible's packed and Skinner's ready to roll. Percy senses the nervous farts in the way their audience shuffles, the shame in their glare, but Skinner's car has eight cylinders and can outstrip any of theirs. So Skinner just waves especially for Leroy, who's benefiting from all those down payments and monthly installments to the tune of 200 percent anyway, since he owns the general store, so what's to resent? An ingenuous display, two Black men in a golden Eldorado, its occupants and their possessions cruising with impunity past a bunch of rabid white boys whose only pride had come from the certainty—now defunct—that the odds were stacked in their favor.

Noland gets there in time to see Percy and Skinner glide past. He spits in their direction and exchanges glances with those in Leroy's crowd who consider themselves his hunting buddies. Glances that mean nothing but derision to anyone who happens to see them; but the sheriff understands—he turns his back to them and walks away.

Skinner has managed to drive the Cadillac over the dirt access road without damaging the chassis. He steers it down to the side of a little house by the river, unloading Leroy's merchandise, gifts for his grandmother, things she's always wanted. Skinner bought her a piano years ago; he bartered his Lab's puppies for it, then nickel and dimed his savings to get it tuned. She doesn't doubt his sincerity or the honesty of this transaction—gossip hasn't traveled downriver yet—and allows him to rearrange her home, placing the television set on the kitchen counter in full view of the eating table, the clock radio and fan by her bed, the vacuum cleaner under it. Skinner's gratitude and devotion are reflected in her musing, this tall, skinny drink of water, now a man providing for her, don't have to ask or say anything, bounty pouring out of him.

Percy's helping, but his sense of balance is off. He can't figure out what's missing, but a humming sound would make it all fit. He whispers, so as not to offend her:

"There's no electricity!"

Skinner is adamant. "It be comin' and when it does, she be ready."

Percy thinking, She be ready? Time it comes, she be dead.

Skinner says, "If it don't, next round, I get a generator."

"Would have done betta to get that first."

# 17

## New Orleans

When Daryl and Monique arrive at the Duvet farmhouse, they find Michael moping all over the couch with the dogs. Beau has not returned, and Mae's hiding out in the bedroom. Michael looks unbudgeable, but he wants to be saved. Daryl doesn't reproach him for having left the island without word of his whereabouts, nor does he inform Michael of his own excursion. Monique roams the room, examining every object—shaking the Mexican rattles, opening and smelling the tin boxes. She's stalking Beau's posters, measuring his age against hers, looking for any resemblance between them, when Daryl broaches a change, a visit to New Orleans to cultivate some of his old friends and associates. His slight exaggeration—he has almost no friends left in New Orleans, and anyone willing to invest would not be willing to socialize with them—does the trick. Michael seems cheered by the prospect. Daryl thought he'd meet with resistance—Michael doesn't travel well. And any talent he has for socializing, in New Orleans or anywhere else for that matter, has never been tapped. Yet here he is, eager to go, Daryl reflects, or anxious to leave.

He adds up the pros: Monique and Michael with him for safekeeping, Noland lost and incompetent, and Arevan spinning his wheels with no distribution to speak of. He can hardly contain himself, thrilled by his own deception, smug with satisfaction as his players fall into place. He strokes

Monique's butt, drawing her attention away from a photo album; she slaps it closed as if to say, Let's go.

New Orleans never changes and yet never seems the same, events both familiar and strange circle with clairvoyant punctuality. A hushed city, it's oddly unpopulated, until night, when its inhabitants' cries of celebration call out from hidden courtyards and dank walls, noise entering its streets like blasts from a horn. Bodies move in clusters, break away and fall back together, vague forms that dance and sing and feed their orifices. The city seeks pleasure like a solicitous host who takes satisfaction in indulging the senses of his guests. At dawn, humidity saturates the light, alcohol has made the animate listless. Then, ancient in its knowledge, emptied of sound, any human voice amplified through a rent in its facade—a door opening or a window yawning— becomes a cry for redemption. Ornate gates guard secrets only the ordained hear. Pass those gates at their residents' acquiescence; hear those mysteries as an honor bestowed or never know them. Families pass on their secret histories in code or innuendo, so the past's cravings are absorbed. In any Catholic city, sin and martyrdom sleep in the same bed. Confession may ransom our trespasses, but longing courts a frenzied passion.

Daryl has not forgotten that his social standing in New Orleans is irrevocably altered. But having reinvented himself, he believes he can recoup his loss. When they hit town, there is no welcome wagon, and precious few to call. Those who are ostracized can never return to what they once were. Daryl has been dropped by society, and no one wishes to retrieve him, for he has become a subject of ridicule. He does not let on, keeping his disappointment hidden from Michael and Monique. Once they settle in a secluded guesthouse at the back of the French Quarter, he throws himself into showing them the tourist attractions and decides to wing the rest. He finds a few from his old crowd willing to meet with him privately; investing in contraband from Latin America has become a standard, albeit covert, cash transaction. More than a few New Orleans lawyers accept retainers paid to them on the off chance that the cash is ever traced. But only one old friend, well acquainted with his trade, is willing to meet Daryl for drinks. Daryl escorts Monique and Michael to a popular piano bar in the French Quarter, chatter lilting over the tables and spilling out of arched doors that open to the street. Cigarette smoke mixes with the cries of foghorns and sax, sounds of boundless grief, held together by the pliable brush of metal on cymbals.

Many of Daryl's old alliances, tamed good ol' boys and untamed socialites, are drinking in the hall. So much of his past surrounds their table and with such indifference that it unsettles him. His mind drifts over pungent streets to old assignations and furtive lusts, all of which he can no longer avail himself. Monique sits beside him, self-conscious, and overdressed in Daryl's estimation, even for New Orleans. He is speaking to David Lee (an outcast for other reasons, but this makes them intimate) as if Monique and Michael were distant aberrations rather than his companions. He can't stop his tongue from wagging.

"You got to see these piece of shit shacks. Some guy walks up to Michael and me and says, 'This place, it's my family's, and I'll be using it as collateral.' So I say, thinkin' it's his family's huntin' camp, 'Very nice, Skinner, right in the middle of the fuckin' food chain.'" Daryl slaps the table, "His family had lived there!"

David Lee regards the pain in Michael and Monique's expressions and cautions him with, "That where y'all from?"

Monique nods yes, her back arched against further damage.

But Daryl's security is in knowing how much he can hurt her. "Now this guy, Skinner? You know *why* he's called Skinner? 'Cause he won a fuckin' frog-leg skinning contest, that's why! Proudest fuckin' day of his life."

"Sounds smashing," says David Lee, distancing himself from the fray.

"Utterly far-out bunch of people. You gotta come up for a weekend, you won't believe it."

Monique responds to David Lee's question from five minutes ago, "It's my home, where I'm from," as if she were stark naked.

David Lee's gaze holds such compassion for her that Daryl pauses—has he gone straight?—but decides it's the noblesse oblige of the oppressed, David Lee's class withstanding, but not his sexuality, that unites them against the oppressor.

"Where Daryl's from, too," Michael adds.

Daryl's lost interest. "Monique, you ever been to Houston?"

Monique won't deign to reply, she looks right through him. Fine, he figures, I don't exist, I'll persist, list all the dope capitals minus Bogotá, "Miami?"

Monique registers his meager frame.

"San Diego?"

Haughty, invincible, is what she'd like him to believe, but if demeaning and idle promises don't work, he can retract. "I'm taking you all those places."

It's what Michael's expected all along. "What, Daryl? No London or Monte Carlo?"

David Lee chuckles—he's developing a crush on Michael's broad chest and burly thighs. Daryl sees it and demeans him as well. "Later, we'll all do that," playing with David Lee, as if he means to include him.

Daryl eyes two of his old fraternity brothers weaving a circuitous path to their table, their dates in tow. Drunk, they bump into his chair, too eager to feign surprise.

"Daryl old boy!" They push their dates into his face like offerings and ogle Monique.

Daryl contemplates their motives: curious about his hick friends, his whereabouts the last few months after the death of the one they now refer to as Little Lord Fauntleroy, the fascinating drama of a scandal *and* their condemnation, which they are ready to bestow now, in the high hope of amusement, believing Daryl's been reduced even further.

The death might not have been his fault, but it only occurred because of his presence.

One of them is appraising every inch of Monique. "And who's this pretty little thing you got here with you?"

Daryl drapes his arm over her chair. "Monique, this boy lives off a trust fund, which is to say, you can't trust him."

"Moan-ique. What say you and your old man come with us? We'll get some sloe gin fizzes, go on down to the levee, and have ourselves a ball."

David Lee puts a warning hand on Daryl's knee, but the man's date is already saying, "I don't drink with whores or third-rate dope dealers."

Stone silence. This is what Daryl likes, anticipation high. He sits back and spreads his legs wide, speaking directly to her. "That hasn't been my experience, darlin'. Last time I was in a backseat with you, you drank plenty. I even offered to get your teeth filed."

Her jock date cries out; he had no idea that he has such a prize. Lifting her up over his shoulder, he clamps his hand on her ass, carrying her to the dance floor. She lifts her head, screeching at Daryl, "You fucking bastard!"

A ring of truth to her description, Daryl likes it. "Bartender, get that lady a drink, and get my table another round. Hell, get the whole damned bar another round, on me."

Michael's drained of color. "Let's get out of here."

Daryl's just beginning to have fun, a few more public

displays and he'll be satisfied. "C'mon Monique, dance with me."

"Daryl, I don't want to."

"I need you to, come on."

Under the circumstances, Daryl can't allow resistance. He clenches both her hands, stretching her so hard that Monique has to rise from her chair. She's not ready for an all-out war, surrounded as she is by hostile forces, but she's close to mutiny when his mood does a tailspin. Depression wells up his face, tears fill his eyes. He's frantic for her embrace to make him whole again. Surprise travels up her features and widens her eyes; she comes with him, permitting him to pull her to the dance floor. The band slides into honky-tonk, but the two of them sway, and Monique holds Daryl together, forgiving his duplicity. They're causing a scene, slow dancing while all the others jerk and snicker about them. Monique supports his shivering frame; he is her armor against the leers. His acquaintances openly laugh at their public display—one Daryl didn't know he had in him. Clinging to Monique, his cheek against hers, her chest guiding his breath, in and out, in and out, until he's composed enough to notice. They're laughing at her availability—his rubbing her back, inadvertently pulling her dress up, his leg between her legs—mistaking her love and care for him as cheap. Monique's not immune to this but she looks up at him as if he's all she cares to see. He catches that smile and kisses her.

From Daryl's point of view, his face buried in Monique's

curls, Michael and David Lee seem wrapped around their table, checking each other out. Michael's registered David Lee's staged posture, the prissy wrist, and his eager eyes. David Lee's noted a deeper intelligence, the wary sophistication under the small-town demeanor Michael feigns. David Lee's plastered a snobbish smirk over his lips to hide the fact that he's smitten.

"Daryl can be extremely amusing, especially when he's being an asshole. What's your connection to him?"

"Old friends. You?"

Monique wants to powder her nose. Daryl leaves hold of her and steps into the shadows, moving in close enough to hear.

David Lee dips toward Michael. "We have a financial arrangement. Daryl borrows money from me. His investments are pure gold."

Daryl should have known David Lee would fall for Michael. Giving all his secrets away before Michael's even offered to buy him a drink—sniffing for Michael's scent, elbow crooked, palm holding cocked head—definitely a come-on.

"You see him often?"

Michael sits back. "Only when he's in trouble, every ten years or so."

David Lee reads sarcasm as flirtation. "Y'all in trouble?"

Michael shuts him out. "No."

David Lee leans in. "Last time he left quite the mess, you know, terrible tragedy."

Daryl snorts. All this indiscretion for ten minutes of Michael's attention, David Lee's staring at Michael's lips, a shit-eating grin on his face, gear stuck in self-destruct.

"This kid thinks Daryl's moving back in on his tiny franchise, nervous over-bred type? So he freaks out, starts playing a stupid game with a loaded pistol. David Lee sips his drink, nudges Michael's bicep to heighten his point. "Silly thing, Daryl always twists things his way."

Daryl calculates that it's too late to interrupt them. Let him hear the whole damned story; it wasn't his fault.

Nervous, Michael scratches his knee. David Lee orders more drinks—doubles. Reckless futility, Daryl observes, because Michael's almost tipping his chair over backward to maintain some distance. So David Lee, in his most ingratiating drawl, tosses him everything.

"Daryl, sport that he is, played with him. The boy threw out some perverse sophistries and delusions—everyone could see where it was going—Daryl baited and played him, until trapped in his own petard, the boy blew his brains out. In front of an entire slumber party."

Daryl folds his arms: full disclosure, against all laws of the chase.

Michael slugs back his drink, cracking the ice with his teeth. "You his business partner, or was that kid?"

David Lee draws back, "Oh, no, no. No, not me."

Michael's gaze moves past David Lee, searching for Daryl.

Daryl has gone to find Monique. She's applying her lipstick slowly and perfectly, ignoring the fact that the two other women in the lady's room are talking about her as if she weren't there.

"She's not even pretty."

"Do you think he got *her* teeth filed?

Daryl's former girlfriend glares. "Why don't you ask her to smile?"

"She must be a good lay, why else would he be with her?"

Daryl enters as both women concur, "She's overdressed."

Monique turns from the mirror. "What you want, baby?"

"Got lonely."

Monique blots her lipstick on Daryl's mouth. "That better?"

Daryl holds Monique. Confronted by his care for her, the others deflate. Daryl gloats in their envy. He's Monique's sanctuary, her desert, and her cross.

Michael's alone and drunk, David Lee's at the bar, his back conspicuously placed in his sight line. "David Lee never asked to meet us. What are we doin' here?"

Daryl smiles. "Noland can't buy enough to make enough without us, and without Noland the captain can't sell. Call it a squeeze in absentia. You ought to know what that's like."

"Squeezing out Percy and Skinner, too?"

"They can deal with it. Know how to stay undercover and how to survive, better than you."

"Well, what do you know?" Michael slings back his drink.

"I know when to disappear."

Outside, horses' hooves clatter over cobblestones. Mounted police. Monique's waiting for him; they're going back to the hotel. Daryl leaves Michael with some advice. "Get yourself a real girlfriend."

There are no tourist shops at the back end of the French Quarter, nothing but wild emptiness and threatening silence. It looks like a ghetto with dilapidated frontage, shuttered windows, and high, plastered walls that close in on the streets. Out by the levee, all-night Greek bars serve ouzo to dockhands and sailors, their jukeboxes playing the soundtrack from *Zorba the Greek* over and over. Daryl and Monique, his arm flung around her shoulders, enter their hotel through whitewashed gates and follow a trail of jasmine down the stucco alley to a garden of magnolia and lemon trees. A spurting fountain sustains the songbirds that sleep under the eaves. The courtyard's a peninsula tiered by two stories of private rooms along the gallery, each room entered through louvered doors flung open to the night. A maid has turned on the ceiling fan and the bed linens are fresh. Monique strips off her department store finery.

"I want to go back."

Daryl sprawls on the bed. "Fine, take it back."

"No, I want to go back, home, tomorrow."

"Can't, no such place. It's what you remember, and no one can. We make it up."

"Daryl, please."

"I'm trying something, then we'll go back. And then we'll go someplace else, make it all up again, then leave again."

She stretches out beside him. "Daryl, I want to live in St. Martinville."

Its people denied her all her life, let it rot in hell. "What do you care? What for? So you can be queen of some Frog Capital of the world?"

Monique looks away.

"You can't go back, baby, I'm telling you. You want a home, want me."

She's soft with tears. "I'm nobody here, and neither are you. But back there you are. In the place where we were born, where I've lived all my life, where they've never, ever bothered to look at me, they finally see me, because they see me with you. They know who I am now. Where I'm from."

Whose loins she sprung from, is what she means, Daryl thinks. Acknowledge she's half white. He lies in their bed, mute with duplicity.

# 18

# Death in Two Quarters

Skinner's asked Kyle to cut the motor; the skiff is rocking and rolling with croaks; two burlap bags are stuffed with frogs, but they are no longer jumping. The croaking on shore has stopped, an instinctive form of self-preservation.

Nocturnal eyes blink before Percy's song, "The darkest day I ever did see, was the time when I went blind."

A clap, then a whizzing noise, and a bullet hits Kyle's back; he slumps onto the motor. Percy's screech skips over the water, its echo slamming into a tree. Skinner grabs Kyle and slides with him into the hull as Percy crawls between the squirming bags, his panic so fierce that it turns to calm. Insects are quiet. Animals hide. All Skinner can hear is his heartbeat and their breathing. It's as if he imagined the shot, but Kyle groans. The soft lapping of waves against their skiff, a bird screaming, and no other sounds: no motorboat, no steps in the forest. Skinner, his hands slippery with blood, lifts himself above Kyle and reaches for the starter. He jerks and jerks the rope, until the motor turns over, its rumble cutting the air, but they've drifted too close to shore and the propeller hits the riverbed, grounding them. Skinner slides down and looks to Percy, he's closest to the oars. Percy's movements are calculated to keep the silence, as if that will render him invisible. He lifts an oar and rises, a dark silhouette against the black night. Desperate, he pushes the boat toward the current, slapping the water with the shaft. The forest and its inhabitants anticipate the slaughter. A volley riddles the skiff; bullets pierce Percy's chest and Skinner's face, velocity tossing arms to the sky. A wild cawing from the forest is barely discernible, a bird calling its own. Three ski-masked men in a speedboat head for an open channel. Their wake laps at Kyle's boat.

There are species of birds that mob predators when their territory is threatened. The sky fills with a swarm, dipping and swooping, wings flapping, beaks hammering. They attack, plunging to strike at the killers, pecking at their raised hands and lowered heads. The night is crowded with long wings. One of the stalkers revs their boat's motor, cutting a swath through the swirling mass. A spinning propeller whisks the three men, their ski masks ragged around their faces, toward the channel. They are not pursued. Birds have boundaries they will not cross. The alarm fades. Only the skiff with bloody bodies remains, drifting in muddy water.

Daryl coughs; some asshole's trying to knock his door in. Monique's arm is flung over his stomach; he disengages and crawls out of twisted sheets to open it.

Michael's sweating and his party clothes are rumpled. "Kyle's been shot. Percy and Skinner are dead. We're going back."

"Hold on. Get on in here." Daryl pulls Michael into the room.

Michael's scream sounds like a bell. "Kyle's been shot; Percy and Skinner are dead!"

Daryl's head is clanging. This can't be. He reaches for his bottle of bourbon. "I have to know what happened."

"They were shot down in Kyle's skiff, not half a mile from the island." Michael's adrenaline soars. "Let's move!"

Monique sits up.

Daryl hesitates, why would Arevan do that? "This is a setup, Michael, to get us back."

"What are you talking about?"

"I found that boat captain, down in Morgan City."

"You *what*?"

Daryl takes a swig of bourbon. "Told him we'd cut him a better deal."

Michael knocks the bottle from Daryl's hand, it falls onto the rug, liquor pooling on the floor. "Are you crazy?"

Daryl retrieves the bottle and carefully sets it upright, noting the brown glass, his fingers around its neck. He's numb with disbelief. "Michael, I didn't push him that hard."

Monique swings her feet over the edge of the bed and slumps.

Michael's incredulous. "You went to him without me?"

"Well, I wasn't going to do the *deal* without you."

"He killed Percy and Skinner!"

Daryl finds a water glass and fills it with bourbon.

"Those were our friends! They trusted me!"

"So let's go back." Daryl chugs it down.

Monique says, "Daryl, it could have been you, or Michael."

Michael answers, "Except we weren't there," when it

dawns on him how implicated he really is. "You son of a bitch. You set them up!"

"Michael, I never meant for this to happen."

Michael's lip curls. "You fucking liar! You do this all the time."

"Michael, c'mon!"

Monique's got her silk blouse half-on, half-off, mismatching buttons into slippery holes.

"Monique, he tell you about the boy, shot himself to death 'cause he thought Daryl was putting him out of business?"

Monique stops dressing and then starts again.

Daryl watches her. "He was a fool and sorely mistaken, he didn't know what he was doing."

"But you did. And you let him. Stood by and watched."

Daryl turns to Michael. "I didn't pull that trigger—look it up under laissez-faire."

Michael's almost whispering, "Monique, come with me."

Daryl starts to dress. "It's too dangerous. Monique stays here. I'll leave her enough money." He zips his pants. "You don't know what we're walking into, Michael."

"Because of you!" Michael hurls himself at Daryl, biting his neck at the jugular, locking his teeth into Daryl's flesh. It's Daryl who tastes the salt on his tongue. He twists in disgust, pushing and punching at Michael.

Monique pulls Michael back. "Michael, I'm ready."

Daryl staunches his wound; his plea is barely audible. "Monique."

Michael spits blood from his mouth. "Go to Miami, or

Houston, wherever, I don't give a damn. But stay away from me and mine."

This time, Daryl spits. "You and yours are nothing without me. I could ruin you."

Monique turns on her heel and runs down the gallery.

Michael backs out the door. "You already have."

The louvered door stands open. Daryl screams down into the courtyard, "Ain't me babe. Self-inflicted ruin runs in your family."

# 19

## REPENTANCE

Daryl had been a Franciscan schoolboy, once upon a time; he's read the Bible: *A man who claims another man's blood will be a fugitive until death.* He's done this twice over. Cain became a fugitive and a wanderer. The earth cursed Cain as he tilled, cursed him and yielded nothing, a furrowed waste. He's already confessed his guilt to the hotel room's Bible, its water-stained ceiling, songbirds in the courtyard, and an empty bottle of Jack Daniels, with another bottle of Jack Daniels. The next moment he's conscious, his room is a wreck: the bed on its side, writing desk turned upside down, all means of illumination smashed. He registers the chaos while curled in a fetal position from the floor: it had to have been him. He'd scrawled a Do Not Disturb the Wicked sign on the wrong side of the door. Unbearable, this loneliness, he throws on a jacket and tie over his t-shirt and heads for a neighborhood joint.

A couple are huddled in the corner, twisting on the bar stool to see, Daryl sees himself with Monique. He touches his neck, imagining her kisses as the girl nuzzles in the boy's arms, but instead feels the marks left by Michael's teeth. He almost falls off the stool twirling full cliché between bottle and lovers. The bartender and the bouncer escort him to the street and hail him a cab. He tells them he's a wanderer, that he has no home, a name perhaps, but otherwise, nothing to speak of. They check his pockets and come up with a room key emblazoned with the hotel's logo.

Rolling down the cab's window, Daryl is riding over empty streets. The French Quarter glows neon pink in the early morning light. Evil luck to be out after dawn, no matter, he's cursed already. A drunken group leave a bar—Uptowners from the Garden District, the blue-blood enclave where he used to live, slumming in the Quarter after some late-night fete. They beckon to him and wave, unaware of his identity, a crowd of witnesses. One of them screams, "I'm reborn," raising his bottle aloft to keep himself steady. Drugs mock mortals, to be reborn only to die yet again, a perpetual banging at the gate. Percy and Skinner are dead.

Daryl dies daily so he can feel something other than what he does, but this is what he's come to: countless epiphanies, lost; anonymous loves forged from insatiable, transitory lust, forgotten; heights of evasion—insight spinning from caustic heart, sincerity held in check by double entendre—useless. Having conjured the strength of the Gods, glorious in his presence, roaring in his vitality, terrifyingly absent in his isolation, inhibitions and guilt quashed to pursue whomever or whatever he pleased, this is what Daryl's come to understand: a stunning assault on the senses, debauchery. An endless entanglement, rising only to sink after each enchanted tailspin, as if his body were torn inside out, the pain his pleasure, too, because perhaps its measure could procure his redemption. A desperate assault on despair, debauchery, because the god of ecstasy has no memory, but Daryl does.

Back at his hotel room, a maid has left a neatly tallied bill for damages from management on the nightstand: the proverbial, "Dear Sir, It has come to our attention." Daryl returns the courtesy on the hotel's stationary, "So sorry, situation out of control, too deep in mire." He has unwittingly instigated the murders of two men he truly liked. He calls room service for another bottle. *The wicked flee when no one pursues, and idols have noses yet cannot smell.*

From the dirt drive that leads to its door, the Duvet farmhouse looks abandoned, except for the smoke emanating from the metal flue on its roof. The sheriff parks his car behind Michael's pickup, blocking its exit.

Mae stands in Michael's place at the oven, one hand on an aproned hip, the other poised with the spatula: flapjacks flipped, eggs frying, coffee perking, Beau's plate full. They've heard the car door slam; footsteps shuffle through the mud and stamp up the back stairs. The sheriff knocks on the screen door, his fist rumbling the mesh; the sallow droop of his features distorted as he leans in to see. At the sound of his car, Michael's black dogs came barking up from the bayou to nip at his heels.

"Matthew, come on in!" Beau is eager to display Mae's care. "Want breakfast?"

Matthew has had his hours ago and says so.

Beau points his fork at the seat by his side. "Sit on down, Matt, have some coffee."

Mae pours coffee for both men; her eyes entreat Beau so long that the coffee almost spills over Matthew's mug.

He waits until she's back by the stove to strike, "Beau, how much you know about Michael's drug dealing?"

Beau's been expecting this. "Not nearly so much as you."

Matthew sips at the rim. "He around?"

"Michael's gone to New Orleans, he forget to tell you?"

"He don't confide in me, Beau. When did he leave?"

Beau instinctively leans back. "Couple of days ago. What can I do for you, Matthew?"

"Are you his supplier?"

Beau's laugh is from the belly, coughing up his windpipe.

"It's not a trick question, Beau."

"You've met every dealer from St. Martin to Plaquemines Parish. Got their phone numbers memorized, so you can keep them in line without getting off your butt. You'd know if I was."

Matthew turns still. "Whole new crowd comin' in with the oil platforms, mixed, real international. Or could be somebody you know, some musician friend."

It takes some time for Beau to answer. "I see, more specifically a colored musician friend of mine."

"That's how I see it."

"What do you want, Matthew, me or my 'friends'? We're clean due to a slight change in our notion of mortality. You'd have to plant it on us. Better hire some help."

"Can't have ecstasy all the time Beau. You're not supposed to have it 'til you die."

"Ecstasy? I don't, Matthew. Mae, how about you?"

Mae's slumped by the sink, her eyes locked on a greasy skillet, her mind numb with dread.

"Two colored boys are dead. Rumor has it they were working for Michael." Matthew watches Beau, sniffing for damage.

Beau reveals nothing. "Who are they?"

"Young, foolish kids, you don't know 'em."

"So, you don't think I killed them."

It's the sheriff's turn to chuckle, his eyes skimming the room for telltale signs. "Not directly."

"You blaming Michael for this?"

"No, I'm blaming you for his actions. You always let him do your dirty work, took care of your folks, keep this home for you. All of a sudden, you're back for an extended visit, maybe for good, and he's got big plans, too big."

Beau, angered by Matthew's intimacy with his family, purses his lips.

Matthew isn't done. "Overstepping his bounds. That's what Michael's doing, something he learned from you. Or something he's doing to impress you."

Beau stares him down.

Matthew rises to lighter air. "Michael follows the rules: if things get messy, he gets to clean up."

Silence, hardly breath, from the breakfast table.

"I'm giving you the opportunity to do something for

him. You've been arrested for possession before, won't come as no surprise. Say you knew these boys were dealing."

Beau snarls, "Something for you, you mean, be your scapegoat, throw the onus on me and two young Black men can't defend their reputations 'cause they're dead. Michael's loved in this town; you can't touch him."

Matthew's ready to go. "Help him settle this, Beau. Otherwise, it'll turn into a kill-or-be-killed business, and Michael's not a killer. And call off the damned dogs while I get to the car."

Mae's gaze sticks to the window screen, her knuckled fists support her frame. The mesh hazes the scene before her; Beauty is racing toward the sheriff. Matthew slams his car door shut just in time. She snaps at the tires.

Beau registers Mae. "What the hell you gaping at?"

Michael's racing his skiff down the Atchafalaya, past where levees guard the riverbanks. Monique's safe in her cabin, packed in tight among neighbors. She cautioned him to stay within the boundaries of his community as well, but Michael has a plan. Each time he comes to a tributary, each subsequent bayou is more remote, more difficult to detect, until he seems in the middle of nowhere. Submerged tree stumps bump and scrape his boat's hull. Michael swings the skiff half circle into an inlet so dense with foliage as to render the bayou invisible.

The houseboat rises and falls in the channel. Noland's anticipated Michael's arrival and is hiding inside the barge with a loaded rifle. Michael guides his skiff up to the helm; a white ibis flies before him like a flag of truce. Noland listens for the motor to subside, cocks his rifle as Michael's boat bumps the houseboat, and waits for his steps to tread the deck. No skiff reveals Noland's presence because he's driven to the campsite through fern and pine. Michael thumps over the planked deck, checks out the warped windows boarded with plywood, but what seems empty is not, and he hears the will to stillness. He tries the door; a rusty screen hangs off its frame, the knob turns, but the door's jammed shut.

"Noland!" Walking around to the stern, Michael spots the sun's glare reflecting off the side mirror on Noland's truck. Parked under cover of pine boughs, it holds a foreboding emptiness.

"Noland, where are you? Are you all right?"

Inside, Noland stands armed and confused; his features are swollen, his face and hands cut, the remains of a beating and worse. His ruse, so easily sensed, feels ludicrous. Michael, his voice innocent and hollow, is alone.

"Noland, it's me, Michael, open up!"

Noland leans his rifle against the wall and opens the door to find Michael pointing a .45 at his chest. Cursing, he backs into his lair, hands raised. "Michael, I didn't kill those boys, I swear it." A blatant lie, "I'd never do that!"

Michael notes the jagged puncture wounds on Noland's hands and swollen face, the disjointed, black and blue nose. He smells Noland's sweat and sees him edging toward his rifle.

"I'd never do anything to hurt you, Michael. You know that. We've known each other since we were kids. Look at me, God." Noland was so careful with his arrangements that he forgot his painkillers, the dullness wearing off, the pain shooting up his nose.

Michael's uncertain. "You got here early."

"Had to bring the truck, came up the back way," Noland confesses. "There's nowhere to go, Michael. I can't even stay here for long."

It's the traces of Noland's beating that toss Michael's judgment.

Noland's shaking, tears water his cheeks, so addled that he's convinced himself. "I had nothing to do with it, I swear. Look what they did to me." He sways like a pendulum.

Michael catches him, his gun dangling by Noland's side.

And Noland is such a mess that he can't do a damned thing. "Let me sit." He slides his way down the wall to the floor so he can concentrate on struggling for breath, figuring himself for a coward.

Michael holsters his gun and picks up Noland's rifle.

Hate flickers across Noland's face, but Michael doesn't see it. He's picking cartridges from Noland's gun barrel, filling his pocket with bullets, and checking the gauge.

"Can you arrange a meeting?

Noland dries his eyes, disgusted with himself. "They'll most likely try to kill you, Michael."

"Maybe."

"I didn't want things to turn out this way."

It's Michael's turn to lie, "So help me turn things around. Set up a meeting."

Daryl is awake, the bed sheets twisted around his legs. His mind is soggy and his thoughts are dull, but his senses are painfully intact. Predictions have shifted beyond his reckoning. How could he not go back? What was left? To make himself up again with the same old story in some same new setting again, alone, unloved, unloving? You can't not go back: *The land on which your foot trods shall be your inheritance.* Daryl's traces fall across the Atchafalaya to sweet cane fields rooting in sand, stalks rustling on silt. His land lies below sea level. There is no solid ground. His feet have slipped in mud and mire and that's his inheritance. He sinks to rise.

He drives a hair's breadth above shallow waters, his headlights sweeping the ancient trunks that line the causeway. He has no plan this time, no other design than to head straight for the old slave quarters with their cabins scraped by age. When he strolls into Monique's kitchen, she acts as if he weren't there, cooking greens, frying catfish, intent on dipping the fish in flour, her hands white with dust. She's wearing one of his button-down shirts over her jeans. Pink half-moon fingertips drop the filets into hot oil, the fish turning crisp and gold. Daryl's stomach rumbles.

She rotates the fish, scraping the crackle off the bottom. "You got something to tell me?"

The words stick in Daryl's throat.

"Come all this way to say something, you better say it. You don't got long."

Daryl wonders who's coming to dinner but "Where's Michael?" is all he says.

"If it's Michael you've come for, why not try his place?" Monique looks at Daryl. "Can't ask for food, can't eat. Can't tell someone what you feel, can't get a response."

He walks to the side window and stares into the neighbor's kitchen. A woman, hazy through the screen, prepares chicken, patting its butt like a baby's. On her porch, children run up and down the stoop. She cuts the chicken's carcass with a butcher knife, and rolls the pieces in flour, mirroring the scene behind him. Daryl imagines the windows beyond her, like stars, dark hands and pink nails, furrows thick with pasty flour, rolling and kneading the universe. A faith bigger than his, he knows, because hands like those fed and nurtured him.

"Okay, so I love you. Now where's Michael?"

# 20

# THE TRAITEUR

A harvest moon lights the scene: a blue plastic Virgin Mary pops out of a matching blue kiddie pool; sparrows bathe at her feet, dropping from a trellis of roses. Crickets, lords of the night, sing. Daryl knocks at the door of the trailer home. It's propped on cinder blocks, a trailer going nowhere unless its haulers were to dismantle the screened-in porch nailed to its side. A posted sign, MUTUAL INSURANCE, hangs at the front entrance. Daryl calls out, but there's no answer; the door is locked. A traiteur lives here, one who provides chants and herbs for the sick, cures warts by winding knotted string around wrists and ankles. He charges nothing—an old-fashioned shaman for whom healing is sacred—but he does barter services for baked goods and live chickens, and he sells insurance, all prophecies and cures indemnified.

Daryl walks around to the back. An elaborate menagerie clutters the compound: live chickens strut in pens, plaster deer decorate the lawn, plastic flamingos stud the vegetable garden; cement rabbits, frogs, and turtles protect the flowerbeds. Chinaberry trees brought to Louisiana from Haiti shade the trailer. Robins are gobbling the yellow berries hanging from their branches, drunk from the juice; they keen around the make-believe zoo like tops. A millionaire would have bought the view if he could find it. Beyond the yard, an overgrown field stretches out into the twilight, a twisted old oak at its far edge. Ancient rusty pickups and an old Chevy, hoods braced, guard the field's entrance. Daryl left his car out front among the more functional vehicles parked in the ditches on either side of the highway. The twisted oak at the field's end centers his vision: figures are moving under its branches.

Only the terrain, a field of weeds below the evening's first stars, separates Daryl from charity or hate. Will he join his group from the camp for retribution or suffer full blame? He must cross this field, keep his feet from tangling in the vines hidden under its grasses, and join these men who may now, depending upon Michael's word, consider him their adversary rather than their ally and his sojourn will be over. Daryl places one foot in front of the other and circulates his thoughts with the sound of their voices, his wishes with their movements. Night falls. Darts of fire, matches, light cigarettes. Kinetic gazes watch him come. Daryl enters the circle of men, some are wary, others are curious, and a few extend hands in greeting. Daryl clasps palms: there seems to be no blame attached to their touch, but he can't believe this. Michael's been watching Daryl's approach, the plodding march toward judgment, and waiting for his gaze to find him. When it does, Michael does not return his salutation; his eyes are veiled, his mouth set in distaste.

A ceremony is in progress. Kyle lies at the men's feet like an offering, his torso bandaged, his eyes blinking at the night sky. The traiteur is cutting the earth around Kyle's perimeter with a bowie knife. Daryl kneels to get a better view. The traiteur and the oak tree both look gnarled by age.

Daryl clasps Kyle's hand. "Hey."

Kyle's grip is strong enough, but he won't speak. The traiteur slices the earth, grasses turning to dark loam; his hands are reddish brown from Indian and African blood, and leathery from smoking the Marlboros tucked in his shirt pocket.

His chant, "What you sow does not come to life unless it dies. And what you sow is not the body which is to be," goes back centuries to the earliest rites practiced on African soil, then brought to ancient Mediterranean grottos. Agrarian rites that were later mixed with Christian exegesis. The most complete extant version in the West has been handed down from the Ancient Greeks. After her abduction, Persephone's initiates searched the earth for their Kore to discover her in hell, whereupon they turned to wine and dance to celebrate their discovery. A deal was struck: Persephone was to reside in Hades as queen of the dead for the winter months—this was the sacrifice exacted for her cyclical return in the spring and the sowing of the grain and its harvest.

Daryl smells the tobacco on the traiteur's breath and inhales his chant. "What is sown is perishable, what is raised is imperishable."

Death to resurrection and the fertility of the fields, Daryl senses the traces: the Eleusinian mysteries, Bacchus rising from the Lake, Tereus howling for his dinner, and finally the Bible.

"Lo! I tell you a mystery. We shall not all sleep, but we shall all be changed."

Kyle's silhouette is complete. The traiteur crouches on his heels for a smoke and points Daryl towards a shovel. "You. Dig."

Loquacious when he's talking to the gods, laconic otherwise. The men lift Kyle and carry him to the Oak's base. Daryl accepts the task before him, to turn the earth within the marks outlining Kyle's form. Above them, many suns, burn like saints. He constricts his throat to confess and plead for mercy, but a voice within whispers, "Fool, why'd he choose you to dig this grave? Because it's yours." Daryl shovels the earth as Michael monitors his progress. Daryl has one objective, to catch Michael's gaze; he strains each time he pitches, the dirt flying beyond the perimeter, loose earth crumbling back to earth, but each time Michael's unwilling to acknowledge his shame. The men relax, soothed and mesmerized by the refrain of metal stabbing dirt, soft plop of mud hitting mud, and the return to clanging shovel, pliable earth. Daryl's breath is heavy, and he's sweating like a pig. When he's done, he plants the shovel into the earth and waits to see whose rifle—Michael's most likely—has been chosen to pierce his being. The men sit in small groups, their soft murmurs blend with the insects' songs.

The traiteur rocks and rises from his heels. "When this soil turns green, Kyle will be well again." He hugs Michael. "Send your daddy my blessing."

The voice inside Daryl cries out, "Bless me!" He doesn't

repeat the plea out loud; he has no right to ask. The traiteur takes Daryl's hand, smiles over the blisters rising on his palm, and tells him he'll have a long life. All that time to remember and Daryl understands: his sin bears the seed of its own revenge.

They walk back across the field, Michael sidling up beside him. "He's mostly for warts and catching wayward goats. That's what he cures. You ought to go to him."

They walk together, part of a pack, like animals the way they sense each other's movements. Arms swing, lithe strides carry them over uneven ground. Soft grunts exhale thoughts, their sighs recollections. When they reach the road, Michael and Daryl stand in silence. Hands wave away insects, headlights sweep over mute goodbyes, and motors recede like lullabies before Daryl turns to Michael.

"So what now?"

# 21

# WRATH

Beau is pacing himself into a shifting fury of resentment and anxiety. It's been two nights since the deaths, and he won't rest until his son returns. When Michael does, craving sleep and a house free of interrogation, he gets Beau, standing square before him, screaming with relief, barking recriminations.

Michael tries to slip by with, "I'll take care of everything."

"Like you took care of those two dead boys? Off in New Orleans while they were killed."

Michael escapes down the hall, from Beau's position at the head of the passage, he seems a stunted, skittering creature.

Desperate to hold him, Beau flings at his back, "Sheriff was by."

His words stop Michael at the staircase, the landing that leads to his bed unattainable now until he hears what transpired.

Beau repositions himself in the hallway. "He thinks you're working for me, that I set you up."

Michael takes a seat on the stairs and snorts.

"He knows that ain't true; he's trying to scare you."

"Who're you working with?"

"It don't matter."

"Matters to me if you're killed, Michael."

"We both know everybody involved, all my life. They ain't goin' to kill me."

"Daryl part of this?"

Michael scoffs. "Daryl's in New Orleans. Expect to see him again never."

"I've told you before. You don't listen. A white boy's got no right dealing drugs to Black folk."

"You did it."

"I gave it away, and I sold it to cover expenses. I used it to suck my way in, play real music with real musicians. I was makin' a fool of myself. Any Black man knows a white man, intending to or not, spells ofay for foe, and you just proved it."

Michael rests his head on the banister. "You never told me what happened, how you got arrested."

"Next time you really want to know, ask."

"I'm askin', now."

"It's a lesson I should have taught you a long time ago."

"Just let me hear it."

Defense lifts Beau's chin. "Happened in this glorious old dump called the Blue Moon, the hour of my disgrace."

"Man, you always go for the drama."

"It wasn't, it was pathetic. Arrested me in front of everybody, laughed 'cause all they could find were three tiny reefers hardly worth mentioning. Matthew displayed them to the crowd with his pinky finger in the air. Knew they were ruining my life for nothing, for a joke. Closed the place down day after I was arrested, left it abandoned whole time I was upstate, a reminder to all us transgressors."

"That place burned down."

"My message to the righteous sons of bitches threw me in jail. After I got paroled, made me a bonfire, heated up the sky from all the way to Lake Charles, sparks flying over Erath clear to Opelousas."

Michael laughs quietly. Beau would like to take his son in his arms and keep him safe.

"So come on, what was it like?"

"This place? It's where you went to get things you couldn't get anyplace else. Hear music white people rarely got to hear. White girls got their dates drunk just so they'd take 'em there. 'Cause once you were there, you were cool, and you got to see who else was hip."

Michael's exhaustion acts as a cocoon. "People carry weapons?"

"Yeah, sometimes. There were knife fights, but mostly there weren't." Beau entertains to keep his son by his side. "It was where women shimmied and men shook, fast, loose—"

"Like Richard's."

"No. Hotter. It doesn't happen anymore."

And Michael thinks, No, according to you it don't, and I'll never play music like you, never be as wild as you, but he bites his tongue because not in the wildness, some demon inside Michael disallows any joy or exultation, but in breaking the law and getting away with it, he's already far surpassed Beau.

"It was a secret society, Michael, allowed as long as nobody acknowledged it, but to me, it was my life. I flaunted it. It's not cool to cross the line, consort with the other side, get high and then brag about it, that's sedition. That's what they punish you for. The lawyers and the cops and the townspeople disgraced me because I acted like I was above their laws and their judgment. You understand what I'm sayin'?"

Michael reflects, Same old beaten-down Beau, acts like he knows more than anybody, making himself a hero, telling his story like nobody's heard one just like it yesterday, and the day before that, and the year before that. Sorry failed old story with no place to go.

"It don't apply to me. I stayed here, made my peace and a place for myself."

Beau hears the scorn in his son's voice. "There was nothing here for me."

Michael rises, screaming, "I was here!"

Beau hugs himself. "I was a ghost, Michael. Whites wouldn't acknowledge me, and Black folk couldn't. You were better off with me gone as often as possible."

Michael hisses, "Who were you, to decide that for me?" and stumbles up the stairs.

Consolation, what seemed so available if only his son returned, flees with Michael. The loss vacuums Beau's heart.

Michael occupies the landing, a gun-slinging, deprecating stance that says, you can't hurt me; I'm stronger than you.

Beau hesitates. "Drugs have no compassion, make you

think you're indestructible. It's knowing that you're going to die, gives you compassion. For me, for instance, I need you to forgive me."

Michael retreats. "I don't hate you; I just need to sleep."

# 22

# THE GULF

*Vengeance is mine*, said the Lord, but word of its possession never did reach Louisiana. The oil market has crashed. The Louisiana coast, last to join the boom, was the first to go. The cost of producing offshore oil could not absorb the glut. Overnight, investors, workers, and suppliers went broke. Michael and Daryl have traveled down to the Gulf of Mexico by motorboat, entering the sea through the mouth of Bayou Teche. Michael intends to kill Arevan, and all other activity has been stifled until he finds him. Daryl wants to survey the extent of the damage, which rigs have been shut down, which operations are still viable, how many men are still working the rigs, and if Arevan is ferrying them back and forth, or if his services, like almost everyone's, have been terminated.

The trip down river was lonely and cold, the levees unpeopled, the bayous empty, but nothing compared to what they find in the Gulf. A thin gray fog rolls over the sea to greet them; monotonous gray waves toss their boat; a chilling mist stings their faces. No other vessels are chopping through the sickening swells; no helicopters are flying into the southern horizon or back to the coast. Foghorns, wailing through the cavities of their chests, have no one to warn. Rigs, filled to capacity last week, toll from side to side on the sea, seemingly abandoned; birds line their decks, calling for food. It's as if Daryl and Michael are the last of their kind to survive.

Michael has taken charge, seizing back his authority by consensus. He hasn't forgiven Daryl, but he's resigned to his return and has accepted his presence as fact, though he's closed himself off from his suggestions. Casual counsel has become the only way Daryl can make himself heard. In Michael's opinion, Daryl made a tactical error; the fatal one was Arevan's. Except that if it weren't for Noland, no one's ever heard of Arevan, not the man, or the name. It's as if he evaporates and solidifies among them as whomever he pleases, which has led Daryl to believe that Arevan will only reappear when he wants to be found. Daryl is struggling, searching for that part of his psyche that has always moved forward regardless.

In his more optimistic moments, he's certain that the economic crisis could work for them. With fewer men out in the Gulf, there is less likelihood of information being leaked to federal agents—where license prevails, secrets are hardly safe—but they'd lose the shelter of a bustling enterprise to cover theirs. Daryl looks out into the mist: he'd have to get faster boats, pay someone in the weather bureau for reliable reports, and navigate under cover of night straight from the Gulf into their swamp refuge. A seaplane taking off from some rendezvous at an operational rig for their lake could be the solution. Daryl's mind is leapfrogging to ridiculous delusions, when the full extent of the damage appears before them.

A massive rig rides the sea, its skeleton crew, sentries left to dismantle, guard, or keep a fraction of the output going, stop their labor to watch the motorboat's approach. Windblown, their helm rising over the waves, Daryl and Michael are careless strangers free to speed past scrutiny, waving at the riggers. The men have heard from those who have been laid off what to expect: the frantic search for livelihood, the threat of homes and cars repossessed, unemployment lines and worse—welfare, mounting debt, and humiliation. Michael's speedboat slaps up toward the sky, lands with a thud on a receding wave, and surges into the next swell, its occupants' freedom the riggers' envy.

Michael is searching the mist for Arevan's boat. He's not the only one who wants him dead; the men have demanded revenge as well. Pre-meditated murder has never been Daryl's modus operandi.

Michael's only response to his objection to a revenge killing was "Price of our authority."

Daryl cursed his own naïveté, for what else could he call it? He didn't think innocence had been left to him, but he now felt it to be a simpering urge. The men were too familiar with the white law to volunteer to assist, and neither Daryl nor Michael would have accepted their offer. Daryl has made a vow to act.

"Of course, first we have to find him."

Michael had laughed, "Or let him find us."

The sheriff has convinced the local populace that drug dealers killing drug dealers is no one else's concern. In fact, according to Matthew, it's not really a concern at all, but a blessing, and this has shamed the victims' relatives into silence.

Noland was conspicuously present throughout the whole informal inquest, and Michael has been vouching for him, something Daryl will not accept. Why trust him? Crazy strategy. Noland has been socializing at Leroy's, rarely leaving the premises, but Daryl believes that he contacts Arevan on a regular basis, more than likely to report on Michael's activities.

Michael begins spinning their boat around the Gulf as if he were on a joy ride, motoring through fog and surf. Daryl chooses the moment to broach his plan. "Request a rapprochement, Michael, say that we're ready to forgive and forget as long as we can keep our economic base. Arevan and Noland can't do business without you; you're the only connection in town." Michael glances at him. "And I'll take care of Arevan and his sidekick, 'The Motherfucker,' after we've located his source."

Michael shakes his head no.

Daryl begs. "Michael, let me take care of this, but let me do it after y'all are set up and running again."

"Remember what you said to me?" Michael revs the motor.

Daryl yells over its roar. "Refresh me."

Michael screams. "I didn't pull that trigger. That's what you said. You know why? 'Cause you can't. You don't have the guts. I let you take this on alone; they'll be munching on you for lunch. Then it's me who gets to feel guilty." And to himself, This is my territory, and I'll take care of it.

Daryl has promised to keep Michael apprised of all he does, but he has not been able to elicit the same pledge from him. From Michael's response, he understands that there's more going on than what he's been privy to.

That night, Daryl drives straight from the Gulf disaster to the plantation, hoping to find some overlooked clue, glean which of his father's rigs might still be operational. What Daryl finds in the library is another disaster. Books, swept from their shelves, lie scattered across the floor; maps have been torn from their rollers; the hearth is cold, the phones are disconnected. News of the oil crash spills over the telex: derricks are idle; Louisiana's seabed is no longer gushing. A few entrepreneurs have maintained their holdings, but the opportunists have abandoned the market, undermining any semblance of stability for the local economy.

Daryl wanders over to his father's desk. Dead center on its blotter lies a newspaper article on Skinner and Percy's deaths: "Murder Arrests Drug Ring." High school graduation pictures of the two young men beam from under the headline. A bottle of India ink has been spilled over the text. Daryl's read the article, it contains no more than what he already knows: the authorities doubt they'll find the perpetrators, convinced they're strangers who are long gone. But the real doubt lies within Daryl, and it shakes him to the core. Michael was not wrong in denying him; he's not sure he could kill Arevan and it's not because he can't find the craving to kill—he's smelled blood, his nostrils have flared in response, and he's felt rage. What he can't tell Michael is that he doesn't *want* to kill anyone. He's been forcing himself to come to terms with what he feels obligated to do, and what he wants. He's unsure, even as he concocts the wildest of plans, if he can continue. He's present yet absent—doubt has stymied him. Daryl wants another life, but the circumstances he's created bind him. And Michael, the one person loyal to him, is the one person other than Monique he will not abandon. Ambushed by his aspirations, Daryl can't see a way out. He'd call on God for help, but he doubts that any god would answer his call. He's wandering in a purgatory like the one he's just left behind in the Gulf. He sees himself act, his mind ticking like a clock, and yet nothing is tangible.

Daryl inspects the room. The taxidermy remains intact, mammals and birds stare back at him as if they can read his thoughts. The furniture's in place and the silk curtains drape over the windows, but the throw pillows have been slashed; there's goose down all over the couch. A message has been left, scratched into its leather cushions; Daryl kneels to get a better view, but he cannot make out the text. He touches the letters with his fingers, the characters long and cursory, constructing each word like Braille: *Set fire to the night. So seeing your light, and hearing your breath, I may return.*

Black ink stains his fingers. Is it a malediction or hex, against him or his father for a past transgression? Creole and African voodoo is practiced in Louisiana; snake healers wrestle with reptiles, holy rollers dance under tents in the backwoods, and born-again Baptists crowd into football stadiums for a second baptism. Even Catholic priests practice ancient rites in their monasteries. Daryl hears a rustling. A great blue heron flaps its wings, not frozen in time like the rest of the taxidermy, but poised to fly, trapped. The library's windows are shut and locked. The bird's garish squawks burst from its throat and its dagger-like bill opens; its wings shaft the air; blackened claws trail behind spindly legs. The air ruffles around Daryl's ears, and he raises his hands to protect his eyes. Fanning the air over his head, the bird flies toward the fields beyond closed glass doors. A sickening thud as the heron hits the glass, its neck contracts and its huge wings fold like an accordion.

Daryl swears an oath to all that lives that he'll do whatever it takes in exchange for its life. A grand and mythical bird lies broken at his feet, the soft gray blue down on its chest is pumping erratically, its legs are sprawled in lewd display. Daryl wants to stroke its scaly feathers, but he'd only demean the creature. The bird's red-rimmed eyes watch his every move. There is only silence as Daryl ties back the curtains and opens the French doors. He's seen birds before that were stunned by glass thinking they can fly through it. They lie as still as death until they come to, unless their neck breaks. This one took it in the chest; its neck is not twisted. They wait with the breeze, the bird still, Daryl pensive. Birds only stand and fly when you turn away.

If not for his pride, Daryl wonders, could he go to his father and try to ameliorate the past, bury the feud? He's witnessed Joseph's unearthly solitude. His resources will survive the crash; Daryl's been the recipient of his acumen and felt its sting; but his own survival is another matter. Soft air brushes his cheek, and he glimpses blue wings fly into a black sky.

What Daryl really needs is some of the traiteur's healing. The dearth of drugs has sapped his reserve and his strength. He's been rationing his stash, staying clean for a day, ingesting smaller and smaller amounts on subsequent days. Surges of useless energy are followed by debilitating exhaustion, his sleep fitful, his anxiety mounting. He listens as Michael and Monique whisper in circles around her cabin, believing he's asleep. Michael sneaks off to meet with whomever, Noland, perhaps Kyle, Daryl's not sure. Michael remains intractable and Arevan can't be found, an impasse that contains a deadly calm. Not so at the traiteur's, where people come and go as if at a bus stop. Daryl returns to him later in the evenings, when they are less likely to be interrupted. The traiteur keeps his trailer so hot that they stick to the red plastic sofa, shifting and ungluing their thighs from its surface. The old man has read the Bible backward and forward, wisdom

Daryl covets. He is consumed by doubt: if he performs this act of vengeance and kills Arevan, can he come back to the world of light? After what he's done, and what he must do, how can he transform himself into the man he wants to become? He asks none of this directly, but obliquely.

The traiteur points to sinful characters beloved by God so that Daryl does not feel excluded or hopeless, reminding him that God marked Cain to protect him from the vengeance of others. Daryl doesn't believe this intelligence has reached his counterparts. The traiteur asks Daryl to consider that the Tree of Knowledge bears forbidden fruit, and most importantly, to bear in mind that its full title is the Tree of Knowledge of Good *and* Evil. The snake, phallic oracle from Hades who seduced Persephone as well, posited this allegory for Eve: *You will not die; rather, when you eat it, your eyes will be opened and you will be like God, knowing both good and evil.*

But God punishes those who sin; the traiteur is sure of this. Animals were herded into the ark two by two, as the story has been relayed—one pair each of the unclean species, but seven pairs each of the clean species boarded the ark not only for preservation but to serve as sacrifice and food, for sin can only be redressed through a sacrifice. After the flood, Noah, like Dionysus, another survivor of the deep waters, planted a vineyard to give thanks.

Daryl interjects: So man could drink himself into oblivion and forget that he is violent by nature? For if man is formed in his God's image—God's spirit, man's breath—

then there can be a violent world only if there is a violent God. Suppose the beating drums at night are our hearts, not warning us but calling to us? Then we must long for hell as much as we long for heaven, and surely—Daryl seems fortified by his next thought—we can step from heaven into hell, and back again.

When Persephone was returned from hell for her cyclical time on earth, her mother, Demeter, goddess of the harvest, promised what is reiterated in Genesis: While the earth remains, seed time and harvest, cold and heat, summer and winter, day and night, shall persist: did that not indicate the marriage of heaven *and* hell?

The next time Daryl drops by the trailer, the traiteur seems distressed and postpones their debate by resorting to homilies: "Never look at a new moon over your left shoulder." And "Don't dig in the ground on Good Friday or the ground will bleed."

He is trying to tell Daryl something by way of allegory, as if he can't divulge what he foresees. His final admonition, "Don't tell a dream before eating unless you want it to come true," fills Daryl with dread.

# 23

## ABADDON

An uncanny premonition, because Daryl has been having a recurring dream that he believes comes from sleeping in daylight. In his dream, they are drifting, Michael, Monique, and Daryl, their boat crossing a wild and empty Gulf. Their destination is always the men on the rig whose faces fluctuate in faint light, as if their souls are trapped in a transitory sea. Each time Daryl wakes in fear.

The day after the traiteur's warning, the dream comes back to him. It begins with Daryl standing on an enchanted beach, his feet sinking into warm sand. He's captivated by the hypnotic curve of its shore, the surf sucking him into its whirl. Restless waves swell to rise, recede to foam, and swell again.

Beyond the coastline, Michael appears in his silver skiff, his boat is caught in an eddy and twirls right to left, bow to stern. Monique runs from the shore to join him, her skirt raised to flirt with the waves, and the ocean splashing her thighs. Reaching out to lift herself, she straddles the boat's rail. Her brother calls for Daryl to join them just as two black dogs walk up to his side and sit, not barking for his attention, not prancing in the surf to swim to Michael's skiff, but like split versions of Cerberus at the gates of hell. Daryl leaves them behind and runs into waves, the ocean enveloping him, as he swims to the boat.

The three of them float, aimlessly drifting toward a gray horizon that creeps to meet them. The boat skims the deep, the bright sky retreats, and they enter the mist. Their faces are shadowed by vapor, and boundless foghorns give way to groaning steel until they are upon it. A rig strains against the waves; men line the deck, staring as if they are calling to him. Daryl sees his face observe, in each of theirs, the face of one who has died. The trio glides past the men in silence, their boat a refuge from the madness, and as the rig fades from sight, they reenter the world of the sun. In its glare their silver boat turns luminous and suddenly vanishes. The three stand on water, laughing at their feat. The sun sparkles, blinding their view of the sky, illuminating the sea, teasing Monique. Reaching out toward a stream of light, she sinks, disappearing into the ocean.

No longer buoyant, Daryl treads swells, his legs wildly kicking and his arms beckoning. The dream will not end, though he wills it to, he fails. Minutes pass, and Monique does not resurface. Michael and Daryl search the waves for her, alarm lingering between them. They dive into the opaque water and open their eyes to a roaring inexhaustible volume, but no Monique, and stinging from salt and cold, they each rise to ask, Where? A groaning sound hisses with the wind, and like divers searching for a snagged anchor they descend again into the sea. A deep current almost drags Daryl in its grasp. Waves force suffocating brine down his nose. Surfacing, he sees the two of them in the distance:

Michael cleaves to air, gulping in amazement, struggling to hold Monique, who is too panicked to sense that in grasping at his neck, climbing to reach air, she's strangling him. Daryl swims toward them; time seems motionless. Michael pits his strength against the sea's; he is straining to save Monique and himself from Monique. His eyes, bright with adrenaline, cold with fear, plead to Daryl. When Daryl's a few feet away, Michael tears Monique's hands from his neck and shoves her to him. Daryl swims toward her dog paddle, embraces her waist, and she calms. Her arms do not constrict his throat but rather circle his neck like a charm.

Dragged down by exhaustion, Michael stops struggling. There is no lifeguarding brace of an arm around his chest as Daryl's does Monique's—only Michael's arms reaching to heaven and water pouring into his grasping mouth: he's drowning.

In his dream, Daryl turns away. He cannot watch. Remote with logic, he chooses; he can't save both Monique and Michael. Tacit between them, Monique and he do not look back. He sidestrokes, Monique in his grasp, swimming toward the horizon, in the opposite direction from the haunted rig.

Daryl wakes to sunset, dislocated, his heart frozen in anguish, his body soaking in sweat. The paneled walls of Monique's bedroom are shadowed by a claustrophobic twilight, and he thinks: casket. But caskets don't have windows. Outside on the porch, Michael and Monique are talking in muted tones, her voice deferring to his drone. It takes Daryl some time to return from the dream. When he does, he hears urgency in Michael's cadence and regret trailing Monique's murmurs that causes him to reach for his pants.

The truck's door slams shut as Daryl runs down the stairs, his unbuttoned shirt flagging the air. Monique is at the pickup's open window, circling Michael's neck in farewell just as she was circling Daryl's in his dream. Michael has the motor running, and her kiss planted on his cheek. They are unaware of Daryl's presence until he stubs his toe. Monique's "Good luck" is almost lost to Daryl's "Shit!" as he hops in pain. She steps back and Michael shifts into gear, just as Daryl opens the passenger door. He climbs in, shutting the door on a pine branch; needles and sap from the torn twigs perfume the cab. Michael stops the truck. Monique runs after them, yelling hysterically, "Daryl, no! Please stop!"

"Stay with Monique; I'll only be an hour."

An automatic rifle is in the rack on the rear window, and Michael's pants bulge where he's shoved a pistol into his waistband. Daryl buckles the safety belt. "I don't think so."

Daryl's window is open. Monique claws at his door. "Daryl, please stay with me!"

Implacable is how Daryl would describe his response, and Monique, afraid to give away too much, says nothing.

Daryl looks at her. "We'll see you later," suggesting to Michael that they go.

Michael tries again. "It's just a preliminary talk; they're not expecting you."

"What kind of concessions you promise them?"

Michael looks out of the driver's window and contemplates the scenery. Daryl's gaze follows his to a line of trees, indigo on the horizon. Daryl's guessing his only motive is retaliation. Michael turns to examine the insects splattered over his windshield before he swings back to meet his eyes. And Daryl sees what he's known all along: the self-destructive son of a bitch means to kill them all, flouting logic, odds, and necessity.

Monique's prancing with anxiety by his window, stroking the door handle. Daryl's locked his door. He says to Michael, "I'm asking again, let me intercede, apologize. It was my fault."

Michael decides to get on with it; Daryl wants to risk his life, wouldn't be the first time. The truck lurches forward.

Monique runs screaming, "Michael, no!" and "Stop, please," barefoot with no traction, but she leaps onto the sideboard.

"Monique, let go!" Daryl pries at her fingers, it hurts his heart to see the panic in her eyes, her disbelief at his attempt, she thinks, at her safety. Windblown hair catches her tears, and Daryl almost loses his purpose, but it returns before he weakens. They leave her fallen in the dust, bruised but unbroken. It takes him a while to recover, looking back to see her with legs sprawled, sobbing into her stomach.

Michael speeds by sweet potato and alfalfa fields until they come to a crossroad. He stops to give Daryl his ultimatum. "We're not compromising with them after they've killed our men. And you apologizing? That's not happening."

Hopeless thrust from A to Z, he needs to learn to wind, wait his turn, bide time. Daryl asks, "We meeting in a public place?"

"No."

No witnesses. "What's the plan, speed on into the bayou, pistols flaring and shoot 'em dead, Lone Ranger?"

"Something like that, yeah."

"They waitin' on us or we waitin' on them?"

"Whatever."

"They'll pretend to be late." Michael and Daryl like sitting ducks.

"Don't matter."

"You lead them to believe we have backup?"

"Yep. Told them I left word with the Sheriff."

"Do we and did you?"

"Nope."

No plan, chance an ally or an enemy; what a fatalistic, self-destructive fool. Arevan's already scouted the site, circling it until Michael gets there, crouching in wait so he can seem to arrive after he's had a chance to observe their number, tally their weapons—Michael on the defensive, Arevan in offense. Does Michael want to die? Does he care? Daryl wonders more about himself. He lives his life with the confidence that in the face of death, he'll be courageous and still, he does not wish to die yet.

Michael interrupts his thoughts: "I didn't ask you to come."

No, no invitation was extended. Daryl left him once to die alone, dreaming it didn't matter; he can't again. The last of the light has faded, and headlights approach from behind, lighting the truck's interior; a startled horn blares around them as the car darts past. Its taillights fade into the distance, gleaming like rats' eyes. What the hell, Daryl concludes, there might be a certain pleasure in blowing them to kingdom come, probably a certain pleasure in getting blown as well. "Let's go. They're already circling, waitin' for you to show."

"For us, you mean." Michael's pleased. He releases the clutch and cruises down the road as if he's on his way to a stag party, a night out with the boys.

Daryl checks the glove compartment for the .45. "Someone flipped out, Michael; probability is, they'll flip again."

"Yeah, *me*, that's who. This time, they're the ones want to do business, and I'm the one goin' crazy."

Noland steps carefully onto the houseboat in Coulee Channel, shaking with fear. Cattails swish in a gust of wind, and Arevan forms from air, stepping out of the night as if he controlled who could see him and who could not. The deck creaks: Noland blinks and he raises his arms in submission. Jorge's behind him, but his rifle is still slung over his shoulder. Noland can't stop trembling.

"Weren't shaking like this last time, were you, Noland?" Arevan smiles.

Noland's so frightened that he forgets his arms are ludicrously raised to heaven. "This time's different. I gotta live in this community! I don't want him dying. You understand? That boy, Michael, dies, I'm dead."

"I understand," Arevan cackles. "That boy dies, you're dead."

Noland lowers his arms, "Don't play with me, Jacques."

"I ain't." The captain of ferryboats, shrimp trawlers and, at the moment, Noland's future, among others'—throws his head back in glee, "No-land, you too much."

# 24

## SLOUGH OF DESPOND

Michael and Daryl leave Leroy's Landing. Their boat is packed with hunting gear, making it appear to anyone who happens to see them that they're headed for camp and morning call. Michael speeds the boat through a maze of bayous until he finally swerves into his shortcut, soon to become their travail, a landscape of barren trunks and dark waters. Submerged stumps bump and scrape the hull.

"Where are we?"

Michael smiles. "This is my way; nobody knows about it."

Daryl unscrews the cap on the gas can and starts twisting the dogs' blankets, soaking them in the fuel and tying them together. Their weaponry's too meager for Michael's conflict or his. Birdcalls ricochet through the trees.

"What are you doing?"

"This is back up."

Daryl is absorbed in his task when Michael says, "Steer for a minute; I need to take a leak."

Modesty sends Michael forward, pissing over the bow.

It takes Daryl too long to register that the Mardi Gras mask floating in the night—the one with the loping red grin and the darting eyes beneath its rubber façade—is riding in a speedboat with hooded men heading for their stern.

A floodlight illuminates their skiff. Daryl yells to Michael and dives for cover.  Shots fire over his head. Michael looks down: a bullet has burst through his chest; its passage is accompanied by Noland's screeching. "What're you doin'?! What're you doin'?! What...?"

Michael's fallen, saved from the next volley that keeps Daryl down. He crawls toward Michael's shallow rasp, and pulls his rifle out from under him, eliciting groans of pain. He soothes him with "Take it easy. Take it easy," and flipping in place, shoots into the light.

Darkness. Waves lap against their boat.

A voice barks. "Finish them off." The sound of a motor, jumping and stopping, its ignition failing to turn over again and again informs Daryl that Noland is flooding the motor. There's a struggle as someone tries to stop him. Noland whines, "Enough."

But he's given Daryl time to belly-crawl to the gas tank and stuff the corner of a blanket down its throat. He's found the conviction he was searching for. He wants to kill the whole fucking boatload now, Noland included. Daryl crawls from the stern, extending the blankets until he gets back to where Michael lies. Crosscurrents bob the boats, moving them nowhere.

"Start the motor." That's Arevan.

Daryl rolls Michael onto his back and waits for opportunity.

Jorge has his automatic rifle pointed at Noland as if he were a hostage. Noland pulls the starter, the flooded motor chokes and sputters, but they're drifting toward Michael's boat.

Daryl lights a match. Gas-soaked blankets blaze a trail to their motor facing Noland's bow. Flames lick the tank as Daryl crouches. Drifting seconds away, Arevan sees the fire, and Daryl smiles in anticipation, because there's not a damned thing he can do but duck. Daryl rises, clutching Michael piggyback, and jumps into the water just before their motor explodes. Flames illuminate the swamp; trunks turn silver. A freeze-frame through the fire of men yelling, with their arms fanning the flames. Jorge's head looks like a burning effigy; he tears at his ski mask. Daryl, his eyes just above the waterline, sinks.

Jorge's screams ring hollow and distant above them. They've fallen into a netherworld: Submerged tree trunks rise through the murky waters toward the sky above. Daryl's lost Michael in the dive. He floats, his arms wings, his legs flung. Patches of light from the fire illuminate Michael's body. Daryl takes him in his arms—bubbles rise from Michael's nostrils—and then dives deeper, swimming into a darkness so complete that he bumps against submerged trunks. When they rise for air, Daryl kicks up to the surface into a red night. Flames riding the black waters climb onto petrified trunks. It's the oil seeping from the swamp's decomposition that catches fire, roaring over the water. Noland and Arevan, oars flapping, row to escape the conflagration. Noland's ahead of himself, glancing over his shoulder for navigable bayou, but Arevan's gaze lingers, searching the landscape for Daryl and Michael. Michael's skiff is a burnt-out hulk, its stern sunk, its bow profiled by embers. Fires consume air, flicker, and spread. Daryl clasps Michael, his chest Michael's life raft, and sidestrokes deep into the Atchafalaya swamp.

He has managed to propel them, to a sweet bayou bordered by a copse of trees. They've entered a slough of cypress. Daryl pulls Michael out of the water over tangled roots and collapses onto peat. He tears off his shirt and staunches Michael's wound. The cloth is instantly soaked with blood. Sending his breath into Michael's mouth again and again, Daryl finally sees Michael's chest rise and fall. He holds him close and asks, "Did you tell Monique where you were going?"

"Yeah." A murmur, "Don't leave me."

Daryl retains some unshakable belief that if he clings to Michael, he won't die, that if he holds him, he can contain him. His heart beats against Michael's chest for both of them. Michael's breath flutters and Daryl sends him back his own. They're sticky with blood. All around them night calls and wildlife howls.

Desperate to keep Michael awake, Daryl asks, "You want to hear a story?"

"No."

Daryl's faint with exhaustion. "Good, 'cause I can't think of one."

Michael rests his cheek on moss and sighs.

Daryl doesn't know if he can keep him. "I thought of one."

Daryl's rendition of "The Talking Bird", what he can remember of the story his mother read to him before sleep:

*A beautiful young woman with eyes black as opals coveted a talking bird and begged her two brothers to bring one to her. Her merchant brothers, accustomed to procuring rarities, set out on their journey, swearing to return with the exotic creature. They searched the trade routes from Turkey to Egypt but could not find the talking bird. Instead, from the Nile they brought their sister lotus bulbs and a necklace of gold; from Persia they carried peony-colored rubies; from Turkey, saffron and turmeric, rare sapphires and pale jade; but she would not be consoled. She wanted the talking bird.*

*The two brothers set out again, again swearing that they would find the bird. Many weeks into their travels, they were directed to a sorcerer who told them where to find the bird's nest He warned the brothers that they might well be assaulted by evil spirits on their way but not to respond and proceed in silence. When the brothers were stopped by the spirits, they forgot their resolve and reacted with violence. For this transgression, the spirits turned them to stone.*

*After a year had passed, their sister set out to find her brothers. She too met the sorcerer, listened to his warning, and acknowledging that pride has nothing to do with courage but rather with human nature, was not tempted by threats. She turned her thoughts to stone, outwitting the spirits to release her brothers from the spell and claim her reward: the talking bird.*

Daryl is lying prone, his thoughts displaced, as if hovering above him. Branches of cypress lace a pale blue sky; dappled light corrugates his flesh. A watery slip of land by a forgotten bayou cushions his body, the spongy earth conforming to his contours. His arms hold Michael's form; too deep a sleep, leaden cold, Michael will not wake. There is a buzzing in Daryl's ear. In the distance, barking dogs are calling for their master. Another hundred yards inland, a man would sink to his knees in slough. It's an elemental swamp; the sticky seeds of its inception are carried by water not wind.

Michael's dogs have found them. They whine, muzzles grazing his face, sniffing at his wound, and when they understand that what they smell is death, sit on their haunches and howl. Michael is curled into Daryl's side like a child, but flies are swarming around the blood on his chest. Daryl tastes salt and thinks of spray from the Gulf storms surging up the bayous. But it's Monique's tears; she is frantically brushing away the flies. A blurred Kyle, his profile high as the trees, pulls her away. Dark palms lift Michael from Daryl's arms; the loam beneath Michael retains his form. Men are whispering the same mourning as the dogs' cries as they carry Michael's body to the skiffs. Monique stays behind with Daryl; she cannot stop swatting flies, her breath short and staccato.

When Kyle and the men come back for him, Daryl questions nothing—not the strong hands and arms lifting him, not the searing pain traveling up his leg. He can envision Michael's end: Michael lay cradled in his arms, conscious, while Daryl fell asleep, the breath escaping from his lips, useless, as Michael, his eyes darting the night sky, struggled for air. There was no one to caress his leaving, no other voice to soothe or ease his loneliness, only the darkness, the cypress his sentinels, life Daryl's and death, his. Braced to carry Daryl, the men step between roots that arch like flying buttresses over the peat, Daryl's Slough of Despond. Their eyes, sweet black, convey his remorse: while he slept, Michael died.

He looks back into the forest and sees Michael's shadowy form gliding over the loam. He grasps at Kyle's arms as he strains to keep Michael in view. *Don't leave me, I will bring you lotus blossoms and rubies, white sapphires and gold; I will heal your wounds with honey and myrrh, calm your sorrows with sweet incense and jade. Please, don't leave me!*

Michael pivots toward him, waves goodbye, and vanishes.

The fleet of skiffs, manned by Black runners from the island and captained by Kyle, sweep like birds over algae-green bayous, each overtaking the other. Men bend down toward the river, plucking at water hyacinth, and when they pass the skiff where Michael's body lies hidden under a tarp, toss the blossoms over him. Their number, meant to be a threat under the cover of night, becomes by day an act of defiance. The men pass each other with greater speed, racing the skiffs past natural levees formed from the cutting and mounding of old meanders. Cottonwoods, sweetgums, black gums, and loblolly pines, nomenclature like chewing gum rings the men's immediate dilemma: they're vulnerable. Kyle and Monique exchange this knowledge in a glance and plans already formed are executed. The skiffs disperse; the Black men turn past oxbows and sandy pools into hidden canals and bayous and fall from sight. Kyle ties his skiff to the stern of Daryl and Monique's boat and climbs aft, his craft empty now except for Michael under the tarp and the Labradors who crouch beside him.

By the time they get to Leroy's Landing the sun has risen but the dock is still deserted, and the picnic tables are empty. The sign on the eatery says CLOSED. The vestiges of the sign that used to hang by the picnic tables reads loud and clear, WHITES ONLY. There is no irony in the way they return Michael to his own: Kyle folds the tarp under Michael's chin like a blanket; Monique caresses his face; and as Kyle unties the line that binds their boats, he slips with the current toward shore.

When Beau slunk home that morning, not having slept in his bed since only Mae knew when, the dogs had been returned. They charged through the screen door to grunt and lick at his heels, crawling on their stomachs to beg for forgiveness. Beau scratched their ears and held their whimpering heads, but as he looked into their watery brown eyes trouble started to rumble around his temples. Mae was slow to instigate the telling, but once she started, she told him quickly, Beau reeling back, Mae trying to hold him, Beau pushing her away, the last time slapping her down. It was Mae who cried out. He deserted her to tramp into the swamp, the dogs lumbering after him. Brute screams echoed through the grove long after he had disappeared, bellowing over the earth.

# 25

## CANE ISLAND

Monique and Kyle brought Daryl to Cane Island. A bullet pierced his calf during the debacle in the swamp. The rest of the men arrived by circuitous routes, gathering in defense of another potential strike. Too delirious to take control, Daryl lies under quilts in the main cabin. The rains have arrived for the season's duration—sheets of sound, water dripping from drains, sky and eaves; the roof spattered with rain, the air thick with rain, blankets and clothes damp. Men yell over the pounding storm, convulsed with cold. Cedar torches and fires sputter; heat is impossible. Spiders have sought refuge in the corners of Daryl's cabin; the remains of other insects—their invited dinner guests— hang from their webs, confirming his analysis: hospitality, warmth, and redemption are all an illusion.

The traiteur's been treating Daryl, spreading a stinking poultice over the wound on his leg and administers what Daryl can only describe as a revolting concoction, what the traiteur insists is herbal tea. Kyle has recruited armed guards from among the men; they escort the traiteur to and from Cane Island; its rim is a dark circle of refuge. Daryl saw or imagined some crouched malevolence spying on the traiteur's arrival from the far shore. Everything he observes takes place outside his window, his only source of entertainment. He's been falling in and out of consciousness. Blue votive candles light an altar by his bed, a shelf with offerings to the Black Madonna: boughs of cedar, mirrored trinkets, bourbon, and leftover food. His waking hours are spent watching the others from his window, pasting together daily scenarios from the snippets of conversation that take place just beyond his door. Kyle sounds like the old Kyle, guarding the cabin with Monique, more irascible and arrogant than ever. From their tone, the two of them are arguing over who, in Daryl's reduced state, should be running the show, both in contention for the position: Monique's claim rests on inheritance; Kyle's, male prerogative. Daryl's thinking, *male prerogative's mine*, but feeling his competitive juices flow is a relief because what's been playing over and over in his head is "Michael's gone," and his heart aches. Monique is not much help; her anger seethes about her solicitude like a storm looking for a coast to devastate.

He's told her, "I killed him"; he's not imagining this.

Monique shushed him, but he told her again, "I did this. I've brought a curse upon us."

And again, she denied him. "No. You did not do this."

"Does Beau know; does he have Michael?"

She nodded yes. "Rest now," escaping his tears, embarrassed by his weakness.

Daryl strains to make out the discussions taking place without him. Monique is high-pitched, truth not her objective; her speculations are culled from their fight in New Orleans, Michael's pre-mortem confidences, and her own deductions. Her interpretation glosses over Daryl's provocation. It was Noland' and his partner's greed that spurred both attacks, a move to take over territory not theirs to claim.

Daryl spits into a tin cup: In the hierarchy of compensation and control, his myopic strategy threw the balance. When the time had come to retaliate for Percy and Skinner's deaths, he had pussyfooted around the truth: every man on his island was in jeopardy. He staggers from the bed and looks out the window at torches blistering in the rain. His leg is stiff with the poultice cast. The men wear oiled ponchos, water dripping off their garments, rifles slung over their shoulders. They are risking their lives for him, because Michael died, and Daryl was injured—the assumption—defending them all. Daryl's unexpected participation has been aggrandized by Michael's death. The voice in his mind repeating, "Michael's gone" subsides. There is no mercy. If redemption's an illusion, revenge will be his only release. Not one more man will die in his place. Daryl feels like killing. He cracks his cast with his fist and shakes his leg.

Kyle's in the next cabin mapping his strategy like a man used to dwelling in enemy territory, slowly and with care. Daryl stands framed by the door until Monique and Kyle comprehend that he's cognizant, viable, and vital again.

Monique jumps up. "You're too weak, go back to bed."

Kyle won't defer to Daryl anymore. The fact that Daryl's standing suggests that his safety is no longer Kyle's responsibility. Ever the pragmatist, Kyle smiles, curious.

Monique hides in Daryl's arms, hugging him. Kyle and

Daryl speak to each other with their glances fixed over her head.

Daryl confesses. "They've been coming after us because I took too many liberties with their organization, made them paranoid."

"You see who it was?"

"I know who it was; I'll get them."

Monique presses her forehead into Daryl's chest.

"Noland?" Kyle asks.

"Part of it, not very willing—he tried to stop them but failed."

Kyle squints to see that Daryl's resolve is unshaken, mutters some excuse about wanting to walk in the rain, and leaves them.

Daryl feels Monique gathering the fortitude to block him. She uses what used to succeed, seduction parting her lips, "Don't go yet."

He backs away. "Can't leave this undone."

Monique will not stop. "Stay with me, please, until morning." She wraps herself around his thighs. "Let me be your baby." Her tongue is in Daryl's ear; her arms are around his neck, her breath heating his face. "We'll make the most beautiful baby and we'll name him Michael."

Daryl grips her arms. "You were going to let Michael meet those men without me."

"Daryl, please."

"It was me they wanted."

Her arms cling to him. "I wanted to protect you."

"Because you love me?"

"Yes," clasping his neck, "Daryl!"

He squeezes her shoulders, his hand like a vise. "Love make you cruel?"

"I didn't know they'd hurt *him*." She begs, "Forgive me."

"There's nothing to forgive, Monique, it wasn't you."

Monique refuses to see. "I love you."

It's easy enough to put together, after what she heard in New Orleans. Amazing, what we'll deny to get what we want. Daryl persists. "Do you want to know what really happened?"

Monique's eyes glance off his neck.

"Look at me!"

Interminable, the time it takes her gaze to come to his. Daryl's hazel eyes are flecked with gray. He tells her, "What you now see in me has always been here."

She tries to twist away. He holds her tight. "I went behind Michael's back and tried to make a deal without him. They came after us because I went too far. They figured I'd betray anyone. And they were right."

His grip brands her skin. Monique cries, "You didn't mean to."

Daryl won't release her. "I did what I wanted, without considering Michael or you."

Squirming, "No, stop, please."

"It was calculated." He whispers into her ear. "Percy and Skinner died because Michael trusted me. Even after he knew what I had done, he never betrayed me. Covered me with his life. And I let him."

Daryl can see part of the truth, but it's not the whole truth. It was Noland and his hunting buddies who killed Percy and Skinner. He had arranged for their murders just as Daryl had arranged for Noland's failure. A double bind, if Daryl knew, because while he's about to chase down Michael's murderer, he'll be leaving Monique and the men to Noland and his kind again.

Monique is limp in his arms. He releases her. "Minute ago, you loved me. Love me still?"

She almost breaks him. "I'll always love you."

Kyle enters; his timing so calculated that it's obvious he's been eavesdropping. "I've got you a boat, ammunition, and firearms."

Daryl takes a last look at Monique and cuffs her chin. "See y'all later, alligator." He doesn't expect to see her again.

She turns with disdain toward Kyle. "How can you let him go alone?"

"Not my job. They be white crackers and so is he."

Their difference is her prison. Daryl offers her his car keys. "Sell it." Monique will not take them. Daryl hands the keys to Kyle, his only request. "Give her the cash and get her and the men out of here."

"We'll be here, 'til we're certain no one's comin' to pick us off one by one in our homes."

Until my job is done, Daryl thinks.

Beau planted a live oak in Michael's memory. It can't be registered for membership in the Oak Society until it's one hundred years old and only then if its girth has reached seventeen feet, a Louisiana statute. But Beau's choice suits Michael. Live oaks supplied mastheads and timber for boats, Michael's favorite form of transportation. Built into their genes is the ability to endure the salty tides that inundate the Louisiana coast; their roots are impervious to flooding. Michael endured hardships and was impervious to their toll. The oak supports epiphytes—Spanish moss and clumps of mistletoe. Michael supported others and expected little in return. Oaks are often found alone with an asymmetrical growth on their leeward side, a gnarled defense against the winds. Michael was stunted by circumstance. They are bearers of sweet acorns loved by hogs, at home in swamps, and felled by rustlers and smugglers for their wood's strength and resistance. The comparisons to Michael hold.

And Monique? Monique is a woman; she won't be thwarted. Monique is about to soar beyond her wildest reflection, direct circumstance and raise havoc, plant opinions, wage revenge. Her truth is willful perseverance. It is women who foment and requite desire, and Daryl has a long way to go in understanding that source.

# 26

# The Pact

If you were to walk into Fat Leroy's in broad daylight, it would take your eyes a full minute to adjust to the dim. Seemingly empty, supper hours to go, the cavernous warren of checkered tables and cedar booths camouflage the bar in back. The town's entire white male population can be found here—if not all at once, simply by waiting until the straggler arrives. Matthew has center stage; as sheriff, he's attempting to hold court, but obeisance is eluding his grasp. In Erath society, Michael was close enough to its center, that is, Leroy, to count as one of them, and Leroy's upset. The sheriff is sifting sentiment with his usual cant.

"Y'all know the rules, everything from rum to cigars has been smuggled through these bayous for generations, but I protect those of us earn our living within the law. Ones outside its jurisdiction fend for themselves." Matthew deflects the sarcastic glances scattered throughout the crowd by pinning Noland. "Ain't I right, Noland?"

"I'd say you're always right."

"And if he's not?" pipes some wise ass.

"I'm gone," says Noland.

Outright laughter follows his admission. This is a country that thinks on its feet when it isn't reclining.

Leroy's implacable. "We watched him grow, Matthew, he was our boy, and we all knew what he was up to."

The men's sympathy is with Leroy. He has more stature than the sheriff; Leroy can't be bought. But lynch mobs are not easy to rouse without scapegoat or riot; and the sheriff figures he can get odds to fall his way, until Beau storms in, a staggering hub of alcohol and fury, yelling, "This your office, Matthew?"

Matthew speaks to the crowd. "We're sayin' it was a hunting accident." And to Beau, "Leave it at that."

Public spectacle is what Beau's after. "You want me to do your job for you? 'Cause I can, and I will." No one believes this. The fact that Beau's able to stand is considered a miracle unto itself. Beau loses his purpose, keening in grief and intoxication, but when he registers pity on the men's faces, he shifts himself upright.

The sheriff makes his point: "You can say it was a hunting accident, Beau, or you can say it was drugs. Take your pick."

Beau reels back memory: sounds and images diminish, as if, swimming underwater, he could surface and find the sun high in a summer sky, see the black dogs loping after Michael, and take pleasure in ordinary things. A rustling like wings flutters in his ears, but Matthew's voice pulls him back into the present. "We're doing this to protect Michael's reputation. And yours."

"Reputation?" Beau's days stretch before him, unaccountable. "My son's dead! I have nothing left, Matthew." A communal cry wings around the rafters.

Beau hears his chance and grabs it, addressing the crowd. "He was selling drugs! And he could've served time like I did, but to be slaughtered? Delivered back to me dead! Jail wasn't enough?"

His voice circles the room and sinks into the silence.

"Y'all knew what he was doin' and why. For me, for his old man, so he could support me. Never breathed a word—to protect me! Never complained—to protect me!"

Men stare at Beau, hands stuffed into pockets, their feet splayed.

"I'll live with that 'til I die. But I'm taking that murdering motherfucker who killed my son with me to hell!"

A soft hiss can be heard from a corner of the room.

Wild-eyed, Beau begs. "Help me, please! Help me find the son of a bitch killed my boy! I'll be the one to make him pay."

Beau pivots, his gaze circling the room until it lights on Leroy, Michael's surrogate guardian. "Help me!" Beau sobs, wiping his face with his arm.

Leroy speaks. "What Matthew's been saying, Beau, is that the law is public. We can handle this privately."

Matthew's tallied the climate. He takes a long make-sure-y'all-know-what-you're-doin' stroll past Leroy and exits.

Leroy's voice sweeps the room. "Shut the damn door and lock it! Nobody else gets in here; anyone wants to leave, do it now. Anything we discuss will be forgotten; this is a closed meeting." And hesitating, "What the hell happened to Noland? He's here the past three days; we need him, he disappears."

Noland is racing his truck down the two-lane highway, swerving across solid yellow lines. He's scrambling to recover the past after having settled for carrying out the orders of others and assuming status through his proximity to their desires. Noland can't mention his troubles directly, for these are matters, the existence of which, Joseph Monroe has sworn he'll deny. If Noland can't reveal the source of his problems even to the source himself, how is he to broach the subject at all?

He's prepared to throw himself upon Joseph Monroe's mercy, anticipating that he might deign to help him in exchange for his son's life. Noland takes a perfunctory swipe at the doormat and enters the main house without knocking, sweating patches under his arms. He stops at the library's door, procrastinating to find the approach that will swing the old man his way. Upon hearing a terse "Yes?" from within, he knocks for good measure, settling on a genuine strategy of concern before turning the doorknob.

The library has been restored to its natural order. In lamp and firelight, Joseph's face reveals the shadows of fallen flesh, the decadent features of a man who, since his wife's death, has elevated his vices to a discipline. He limits his clients to those with money-laundering problems; owns businesses that other men run for him; floats cash loans at thirty-percent interest; smokes Cuban cigars; drinks Kentucky bourbon in a crystal shot glass; likes his Louisiana crayfish shelled, sautéed, and served with burnt butter and Indian rice; his Chinese teas, black; and his quail with cheese grits. Joseph tosses Noland a disparaging glance from his desk—his eyes are bright from perusing ledgers—as if he's been expecting him or someone of equally worthless demeanor.

Noland's purpose meanders. The fire in the hearth eats the air, moisture films the windows.

"You're son's in trouble, sir."

"Predictable occurrence, Noland. I was under the impression it was you dealing with him."

Noland's so nervous, his foot stammers. "He's in big trouble."

"And you? What big trouble are you involved in this week?"

Noland tries flattery. "I need your advice."

"You need my advice for my son's troubles?"

"I need your advice for all our troubles, sir."

"Are you asking me to represent you? Because I require a substantial retainer."

"I can't hire you sir; that would be ridiculous—" Noland, afraid he's offended, backtracks. "I just need to understand if my secrets are as safe with you, as yours are with me?"

Joseph frowns. "Sit down, Noland."

Noland perches on the edge of a Louis XVI chair for his next intimacy.

"I'm in fear for our lives, sir."

Joseph's cash can't be traced, and he has kept the workings of this particular operation at a distance—two phone calls away, to be precise. He is, however, interested in his son, because, having given Daryl life once, he'd like to think it remains his prerogative to take it or leave it.

"Talk to me, Noland."

# 27

# He Who Receives So Many

Conducting a final raid on his father's library late that night, Daryl finds some files in a forgotten closet; its door was left open. The red light blinking on the phone indicates that Joseph is still conducting business from upstairs. Daryl finds what he's looking for up front, a file sticking out of the cabinet as if it has just been returned to its place. Listed among those mortgaged to the hilt, with his name right next to its number, is one Jacques Navera—the letters are reversed but it's the same man. Navera/Arevan pledged his shrimp fleet to Joseph Monroe six years ago. Daryl can't tell if it has been repossessed or if he has paid the debt. The paper trail leads to Grand Isle and the key to Daryl's puzzle, *Our Lady of Fatima*, Arevan's vessel. He leaves the file as he found it. A rustling sound startles him; he half expects to see the heron, but it's his father who is stationed in the dark. Joseph switches on a lamp.

Daryl blinks. In the light his father seems stooped and ancient. He asks him, "*Our Lady of Fatima*, the one who performs miracles?"

Joseph says, "I didn't name her."

"What do you have to do with this?"

"As little as possible. Unlike you."

Daryl folds his arms. "How much?"

"I dabble in everything worth anything, boy. Maybe, when you get your sense back, we can do business."

Why, Daryl thinks, did I not figure this out? "What do you know about Michael's death?"

"I don't deliver messages, Daryl; I receive them. You and he played too hard with people's livelihoods, can't blame me for what you did."

"No, no I can't." Daryl breathes deeply.

"What're you doing here?"

He scans the room. Light from the hearth fire flutters up the wall. The black-and-white photograph of him with his mother, framed in silver, has been placed on the mantle. "I've come back for what's mine."

"I talk to your mother every night. You got something you want to tell her, like how proud she'd be of you?"

"I'll just pray to her directly, thank you."

His father appears to be aging as they speak. Daryl limps up to the mantle and takes the photograph, sliding it between his shirt and his chest like a shield.

A stench permeates the room. Daryl coughs.

Joseph lights the wicks of scented candles, turns off the lights and sits at his desk. "She comes to me. We speak." Weary, he closes his eyes; his eyelids are wrinkled.

Daryl takes a last look around, at the stuffed birds, their wings spread, their glass eyes sparkling in the candlelight; at the book-lined shelves shrouded by maps. Silk pillows partially surround the bird's message scratched into the leather divan: *Set fire to the night. So seeing your light, and hearing your breath, I may return.*

His father nods, exhausted. "Goodnight, Daryl."

Daryl leaves the way he came, past the host of chairs and the piano—he closes its lid—out through what had once been the slaves' door. He's ready to sever whatever binds him to Joseph, in hate or need, unaware of the machinations being put in place for him.

Shrimp men are reapers. They sail at night with the tide, the wind blowing in from the south, the moon full. Daryl keeps to the inland water route, past Spanish Lake and Vermillion Bay, navigating down the channel toward where the shrimp fleet berths. Grand Isle lies in Jefferson Parish, one of the barrier islands scattered like seeds to the west of New Orleans. A skinny peninsula of homes dangling into the Gulf of Mexico, the Isle has one main road and one channel, thin black lines of transport running parallel to the sea that service the residents and the docks. Vehicular traffic on Grand Isle crawls past stilted turquoise homes and car dealerships turned into drive-in churches to end at a joyless amusement park battered and stupefied by gulf winds. But a boat can speed down its coast in half the time. Daryl drifts south on the open channel, smelling the salty air. The sky is crossed with rigging; masts rise into the firmament. Halfway down the channel, he spots *Our Lady of Fatima*. No miracle can deliver him now; Arevan must want to be found; his motorboat bobs off the stern of *Our Lady* in full view. Daryl docks among the smaller boats at the wharf.

After his talk with Joseph, Noland drove for some time to calm his battered nerves. His present goal is the only society in town, the aimless vigilantes at Leroy's. Noland now believes himself protected by a larger force, but he's sneaking into the bar just in case, sidling along the trash containers in its back lot as he counts the Ford Broncos and Mercury Cougars and calculates each owner's propensity for levelheadedness or violence. He stops to gather himself, relieved to see that the sheriff's car is missing, and turns the corner toward Leroy's neon-pink-and-green entrance. A crusty ballad from the bar's interior clouds their voices, or he might have heard them. Arevan and the sheriff, positioned in full view of the main door, are leaning up against a Chevy Impala as if they had all night to chew the fat. Sighted, Noland blinks. Not fool enough to run, he sees, in angular moonlight and pink glow, Arevan's gunman, Jorge, stationed in the Impala's back seat.

Matthew calls out as if they were best buddies. "Noland!"

Noland saunters over to the car, attempting nonchalance.

Arevan won't hide his contempt. "You're a hard one to find all of a sudden. You locate the Monroe boy?"

"No idea where he could be."

Matthew cajoles, "Of course you have, you work for his daddy."

Noland says, "Everyone reckons Daryl's back in New Orleans. He'd be a crazy fool to show his face."

Arevan laughs. "He is a crazy fool."

Noland's knees are knocking. He's struck what he

believes to be a bargain, not understanding that the bargain stands before him.

Matthew inclines his head. "The captain's come to offer us a deal we can all live with."

Arevan assesses them both, wondering if either one can affect the necessary result, and then decides that it hardly matters. Whoever messes up will accuse the other, and he will simply get a new bodyguard. "I'm giving Jorge to y'all. Offer him to the crazy Monroe kid and his crew as a gift, you understand? Let them have him. They'll know what to do."

This is not the resolution Noland had expected. He ducks his head into the Impala to escape Arevan's scrutiny. The overhead light subdues the night, drawing a whir of moths.  Illuminated, Jorge's face is scabbed with puddles of red, puckered skin that's oozing and oily with sulphate cream. Noland shivers in disgust—"Rougher burn than I thought, Jorge. Hardly recognized you"—and withdraws.

Arevan is savoring his game: "*Venga con* Noland."

A query forms over Jorge's brow; Noland was partly responsible for the debacle in the swamp, what should have been a straightforward shooting. He hesitates, confused by their comradery, but disembarks.

Arevan sheds his jacket, drapes it over Jorge's shoulders, and plunks his cap on Jorge's head. "Don't want you catching cold."

Jorge smiles in gratitude.

Arevan retrieves a rifle from under the back seat and hands it to Jorge, *"Hasta mañana,"* as if they're all having lunch the next day. He gets into his Impala and adds, "Do your job good, Noland; I'll be waitin'. And don't let him kill you first."

Matthew stuffs himself into the sheriff's car with a "Good luck, boy."

Their taillights jump over ruts; their bumpers hit the road, and they're gone. Noland leads Jorge around back to his own vehicle.  No sense LeRoy's crowd spotting them before he can make his delivery.

Noland drives Jorge across the road to Leroy's Landing, murmuring, "*Qué pasa*, Jorge, huh? *Está bien*, chill out." And in his boat, pulling out from the dock, Noland guns his motor full throttle, until the river fans behind them. He keeps to the widest waterways as long as possible. The wind blasting up from the Gulf hits their forty-miles-per-hour head on, permeating their skin. Jorge's so cold he's cradling his weapon. Crossing over into a bayou that leads to Cane Island, Noland reduces their speed and the wind, caught by cypress, blocked by pine bluffs, subsides. It's a brief respite because the rain returns.

Cane Island sizzles. Flaming pine torches sputter. Jorge shields his face; his eyes dilate. Pungent smoke from the pine tar blows over the water. Noland threads his way toward the island. Skiffs, moored to buoys, pitch for the beach. Men, posted at intervals along the shore, lift their rifles and aim at Noland's boat. He flaps a filthy white T-shirt and yells over the chug of his motor, "I want to talk to Daryl."

A voice from the dock replies, "Not possible."

Noland pleads. "You can disarm us."

Laughter. "We can kill you."

Noland offers a pidgin explanation. "We make deal."

The same sonorous voice responds. "We speak English. Give it your best shot."

Jorge's appraised the guards on the shore, their raised rifles aimed at him as the boat putters to shore, and makes a mute calculation, placing his rifle on the bench and raising his arms. Their boat knocks the dock, reverses from the impact, and lurches in the surf.

Noland forgets all about his gun and almost gets shot carrying it onto shore in the insouciant presumption that he's joining old friends. The men disarm and frisk him, then unsheathe a knife strapped to the length of Jorge's calf. These guards aren't particularly threatened by or interested in either one of them, so Noland volunteers his news: "This is the guy who killed Michael, and most likely Percy and Skinner. He don't speak English, so he don't understand what's happening. I'm giving him to you."

The men don't trust Noland, everyone can see it's a sorry offer but anticipating another scene of which he will be the brunt, they step aside, granting him free reign. Noland explains to Jorge, "*El loco, esta aqui,*" and trudges up the muddy incline toward the camp, his charge following behind. Noland is weightless with relief until they reach the encampment. A proud and haughty Kyle waits for him on the cabin's porch—not the diminished and dissipated

Daryl he had expected, who owes him for his lack of mercenary performance in the swamp and would be duty-bound to render his debt of gratitude, however noxious and condescending its application—if not for this cunning Black man who owes him nothing. The runners close in around them, and Noland understands with a flapping, whirring anxiety that the laughter surrounding him, and Kyle's seething contempt, comprise the same vernacular of hatred.

# 28

## BETRAY ME?

Monique's conviction, an instinctive trust in the mercurial and capricious nature of fate—that it belongs to her—flares when Noland and Jorge are brought into the cabin. Her eyes flicker and then glaze over to hide her speculation. She registers the burns on Jorge's face, the ship captain's attire—an ill-fitting prop if she ever saw one—and his surly demeanor. Jorge's slow inspection of the cabin, his feral inspection of her, reveals the instincts of an underling; his nostrils flare; his eyes dart. Noland slides into the center of the cabin, uneasy about whom to defer to, but he widens his gestures to include both Kyle and Monique, his head swinging in her direction, his neck contorting to throw an explanation toward Kyle.

"This man's rifle's the one killed Michael. No doubt about it. Bullets'll match. You do with him what you want. We'll take his death as a sign from y'all, the matter's closed."

Kyle says, "We? We'll leave it."

"You blind? Don't you get it? Him dead solves everything, no investigation, no blame shifting around. Kill him. Say he was trespassing." Noland turns to the men who have followed them into the room, certain that his logic is irrefutable. "He ain't white. You can kill him."

Kyle looks at Jorge. "He ain't Black, technically speakin'."

Monique says, "He's not the one we want."

Noland's indignant. "He killed Michael!"

Kyle shrugs. "Then you kill him. And take his body with you."

Noland quells the precipitous edge to his panic and starts again: "I'm offering you Michael's killer, and you think it's a joke? He's a sailor, a marksman, and he's marked, burnt by fire." Noland searches the room for a landing strip. "Shot Michael at point-blank range in the chest. I couldn't stop him. Michael didn't have a chance."

Monique winces.

Noland pursues her. "Take a look! Would've blown Daryl away, too, only I intervened. That's when their motor exploded. Look!"

Jorge's fidgety. "*Qué es?*"

Noland explains. "*El loco*, the one did this to you. We'll find him."

"*Sí, el loco*," Jorge grins at Monique. "Motherfucker!"

Mirthless laughter from Kyle, "Why don't we kill you both?"

Noland, "Come on, you want to stand trial for killing me? Look at him!"

"Sure," Kyle smiles. "He's just along for the ride, 'cause he trusts you after what you did, savin' everybody. 'Cept Michael. Percy and Skinner."

Noland almost pukes from fear but nods toward Jorge instead. "He don't know, do he? He don't know, or he'd already be trussed up like a dead stag!"

Jorge, thinking to ingratiate himself, shoots an imaginary rifle at one of the armed guards. "Bang, bang."

Noland fixes on Monique. "Take what I'm offerin', Monique."

Monique laughs, "He's a hired hand."

"Who aims to kill your man. I ain't callin' the shots here. I'm just giving you a way out, trying to save our lives."

The rain leaves as quickly as it arrived. Outside, cedar boughs drip. Inside, Noland's prophecy whirs around the room. "He will kill Daryl, because that's what he does. Then you, Monique, and then Kyle." Noland's eyes rove from one runner to another. "Then each of you. Bang, bang." Noland turns to encourage Jorge, "El motherfucker."

Jorge grins in anticipation. "Motherfucker." This time he aims at Monique, flirting, "*El loco*, Bang. Bang."

Noland smiles. "Take him, Monique; he is the one who shot your brother."

Monique moves toward fate with implacable speed. "Let Beau do it. It's about goddamned time he did something."

Noland erupts with enthusiasm. "I'll get him!" Forgetting his place for a second time, barking an order. "Keep him under guard."

Kyle rebukes him. "You'll stay here under guard with him."


Daryl has dozed off in the captain's cabin, enervated by a throbbing leg and the waves rocking *Our Lady of Fatima* like a cradle. Sleep is an unwelcome analgesic, leaving him unprepared and vulnerable. The rain softens the music wafting from the bar at the dock and occludes the car pistons clanking to a halt outside the boat, footsteps treading the forward deck. When the door opens, Daryl hears the creaking hinges and clutches his rifle. Positioned in a cubicle bunk, he's hidden from immediate detection. He points his rifle at Arevan's back and cocks it. Arevan raises his hands and steadies himself on the boat beams. When he twists his head, his gray eyes, luminous in the dark, hold no surprise.

Daryl's derisive. "What? No shadow?"

"He's out there."

"He were, you wouldn't be telling me." Daryl rises from the bunk, aiming his gun at Arevan's chest. "Bottom left side of the heart is where Michael was hit."

Arevan swallows. He'd rather spit but his target's a foot too far. "So shoot."

Daryl pushes the cabin door open, air flows into the hull. *"Jorge, aqui, por favor."*

Laughter from the dock, creaking ropes and rocky sea, then a car door slams, then another, the attenuated sound of tires spinning north, and finally, the stoic rush of water.

"Wherever could he be?" Daryl asks.

He moves forward to search Arevan, patting him down. "Let's go."

"Me, I have friends out there."

"So you've said."

"They'll follow you."

Daryl points toward the hatch and steps aside. "You first."

By the time Mae drives into Leroy's lot, guiding her Chevy over the ruts, the neon sign has been shut off. Music from the roadhouse sifts outside. Pickups and vans, like slumbering beasts, lie in wait. The door flings open; the music swells, laughter following it. Mae takes this as a sign, a siren's call to leave her car. A breeze stirs into a gust of wind. She's present for its birth; it whips her hair.

Inside Leroy's, tight little groups toss cheap shots and bet on whether Noland might yet arrive with some answers. Earlier aspirations have fizzled; nothing's expected to happen. The town meeting has dispersed into groups of sedentary drinkers. The waitress has abandoned her apron and tips to roost on the stool between Beau's legs.

Too tired to wait any longer, she begs the question. "You drinkin' in this place all night?"

Beau figures that he's got the whole listless night to decide, much less respond to her request. He's nursing his spirit with Brandy Alexanders.

"I'm crushed," she insists.

"How's that?" Beau asks. His tape recorder clicks and stops. He doesn't press play again. They've been singing his recording over and over: *You know the reason I'm condemned. For this, for that. It's the fault of my gun.* Everyone knows it by heart, and they're no longer in the mood.

The waitress presses her butt against his crotch. "Because I like you."

Beau has forgotten what they were discussing but he's aroused. "You like that style?"

"I favor it."

Beau takes in, for the umpteenth time, her saggy breasts in need of a halter, the overdose of perfume clogging his nostrils, and calls for Leroy, certain that he needs another drink. Leroy's been darting back and forth between the bar and the phone all night, anticipating its ring.

Morose is the word that comes to Mae's mind as she enters. Men pull back from the bar, clearing a path straight to the stringy waitress, her butt still perched on Beau's stool.

Beau, soggy from the brandy, filters his guilt with, "What're you doin' here?"

Mae testifies to her possession of him, their domestic arrangement. "There's someone waitin' for you at the house."

The men, embarrassed for Beau, call out. "Mae, we've been gettin' your old man drunk." They're propping him up as if he'd *better* be polite. The waitress retreats as Mae claims her spot.

Beau relents. "What can I get you?" But when she's served, and the men have discreetly turned away, he adds, "You have no right comin' here," assuming it's Mae who has been waiting for him at the house, and that this is some silly plea for his return.

Monique had been too jumpy to wait as Mae had asked. Driving Daryl's Corvette, she tracked Mae's taillights, lingering just far enough behind to go unnoticed. When Mae turned into Leroy's lot, Monique turned off her headlights and parked. But when Mae didn't reappear from the roadhouse, trailing behind Beau's urgency as she had hoped, she left the husk-like Corvette to burst through the door, surprising everyone at Leroy's. The wind blows in after her, rattling the windows, lifting paper napkins to surf and settle like birds.

Leroy, first to spot her, yells. "Out!"

Monique is blind to threat.

Her presence shakes Beau out of his drunken state. "This is my daughter, y'all. I want her treated with respect." Beau leaves Mae to stand beside Monique, taking her in his arms. "Darlin' what's wrong?"

Her purpose intangible, she's dizzy. Beau, her need for him so long deferred, has his arms around her. "Beau?"

"I'm right here, baby. You need to sit down?"

When Monique opens her mouth, like a suckling for food, nothing comes out.

Beau brushes her hair from her face. "Come on baby, don't be afraid."

Monique murmurs, "I know who did it."

Beau twists her shoulders toward the male majority. "Do you hear this? Baby, tell them."

Summoning volume and with volume, strength, Monique announces her purpose. "I saw him, Michael's killer. I recognize him. He's here."

The men slump and scowl.

Beau demands their attention. "Listen to her!"

Monique chants: "We have him. We're holding him on Cane Island. Noland brought him to us."

Beau is exhilarated. "Do you hear? Noland came through!"

Leroy breaks the silence. "Where is Noland? Why didn't he bring him here? She's making this up. Michael was out in the middle of nowhere; she saw nothing."

"My daughter don't lie."

The men stifle yawns.

Leroy speaks for them. "It's been a long night, Beau. Everybody's fucked up, and she's off, I don't know on what, having delusions."

Monique tries again. "Noland sent me; he has him. I saw him. I was the one brought Michael back with the dogs. Michael's boat was burned and this man's marked by fire. There are burns on his face. I just saw him!"

Beau stops her. "That's enough, sweetheart." He fumbles in its pockets for his car keys. "Now this is Michael's sister, y'all, and he loved her. So if she even suspects someone, we have to see for ourselves."

It's Beau's omission of *his* love for her that feeds Monique's resolve. She screams. "What's wrong with y'all? What kind of men are you? I know it's him! He's a killer!"

Guilt flaps around the tavern like a bat. Monique sees it in their faces; some are scarred with jagged cuts.

Beau's disgusted. "Y'all made me a promise and you can keep it or go to hell." He catches his arm in a jacket sleeve and punches it out in anger.

But Leroy's by Beau's side, and he's armed.

# 29

# THE SACRIFICE

Kyle has ordered the camp dismantled and destroyed. Kindling stokes the fires, coaxing the damp wood into shafts of steam. When flames boil the last drops of water, winds will feed the fires; blazes will howl with air, cracking over the clamor of men. Kyle shouts directions: what stays, what burns; personal effects are stowed into boats. Inside the main cabin, Jorge and Noland drift from chairs to windows, drawn to the commotion. They are not shackled, but it is a house arrest.

If Daryl were not so intent on the river ahead, he would sense the din to the south. Vapory columns of smoke rise into the night, its shadowy matter pillars earth to sky. But he's myopically driven, gunning his motor north against the current, catapulting his motorboat upstream from Cane to the Red River, propelling them, in his mind, to the less corruptible police in the Protestant north of Louisiana. He's in the dark, even then, as to how much is out of his control.

Arevan, trussed into a seated position, ropes binding his arms and legs—the ends of which wrap around the boat's cleats so if he were to jump, he'd drown—sees the smoking sky behind Daryl and laughs. "What's the fastest way to hell?"

Daryl can't be threatened; he grins. "Take a rope and hang yourself?" The river ahead is swollen and sloppy from the rains. "Or launch away."

Arevan tries to stretch. "Too stifling."

Daryl smells dank air, dead fish scattered by the storm, aromatic wood from torn branches. He laughs. "Ascend and jump, descend and fall?" A bird crashes through the forest.

Arevan glares. "'Bout your speed, no? You're the one who drugged yourself for the highs. Escape everything, remember nothing of what you owe others."

Daryl thinks, a killer, proselytizing.

Their wake churns the river; water levels off and slaps the shore. Any movement in the forest incites showers.

Daryl tells him. "I'm turning us in."

Arevan laughs. "To who?"

"Sheriff's office."

"Betray me to my own? That's rich."

Daryl turns, a perfunctory glance. "You ever hear of the state police? 'Cause that's where we're going."

"Who would believe you? You... a drug dealer!"

Daryl heard the stutter. "You'll hang."

"I won't hang. You want me dead, you'll have to do it yourself."

Daryl says nothing. He wants more than Arevan's death.

"Oh, I forgot. You don't do your own killing, just set everything up, then split. Let somebody else do the dirty work, 'til you don't have no partners left and your profit's a hundred percent."

Daryl faces upriver, racing the boat forward, and deflects his shame. "Yeah, well this time I came back. I'm paying for this, and so are you."

"I get it. Confess and poof, instant absolution."

"That's not it."

"Oh yes, it's true. You can believe anything you want, and you don't have to prove it; that's faith. You believe in nothing. Nobody has any faith in you. You're still only a drug dealer."

Daryl reminds him. "You killed Percy and Skinner. And you assassinated Michael. And it's my fault. I'm turning both of us in."

Smoke travels with the wind. Arevan smells the first waft of cedar. "I didn't kill your Percy or Skinner. Not me, witnesses can prove where I be."

Daryl starts at the news. "Who did?"

"Noland and his hunting buddies—locals did those murders. Y'all got them folk very worked up, spreading cash around to all the colored towns." Arevan nods toward the sputtering sky and orange sparks to the south. "Looks like they be having a barbecue on your island. You off assuaging your conscience; your people be gettin' their asses fried."

Daryl finally looks back.

Arevan smirks. "Your girlfriend there?"

The horizon line is pale with smoke; flames unsettle the night. Daryl twists the wheel without stopping. Arevan is almost tossed into the brink but for the rope binding him to the cleats. The boat spins, centrifugal force clutching it and its occupants, until Daryl revs the engine, and they lurch downriver.

Miles of hell-bent silence back to the island, anxiety eating his heart, Daryl swerves the boat. Too late, its bow slams into a dark square with a massive whack. A Magnavox TV, its screen shattered on impact, sinks at his port. He swears to himself, twisting the boat in place. Ahead lies an obstacle course: a Hoover vacuum cleaner is caught in tree roots and a clock radio bobs to his starboard. How, Daryl wonders, do they float when they should have sunk to the bottom? Before him lies a barricade of electrical appliances—anything that could have been bought with blood money has been hurled into the river.

They are close enough to Cane Island to inhale the smoke. Gusts billow over the river. Zigzagging through the machines, Daryl sees his alternative and swerves the motorboat into a creek that curves to the west. They enter a heavy silence. This is a passage to the island that Daryl's only heard about, as if it were folklore, an access navigable only after heavy rains; otherwise, its waters are too shallow and tangled with vegetation. His boat rides the swollen tide. Wind shakes the branches; leaves, slippery with rain, drench the two men. In a few months, herons will dart beneath the branches arched over the creek. This passage leads to the rookery hidden on Cane Island's northwest corner; an encampment distinct from Daryl's own on its southern tip.

The stench reaches them first. Arevan gags and vomits. Trees, coated with wet excrement, hide the fire-lit skies to their south. Daryl doubles over with nausea, suffocating from the collision of bile rushing up his throat and the putrid air he's inhaled. Cane Island is a breeding ground come February and a nursery by April. By the summer months, when the birds hatch, its where they rear their young. The chicks eat, regurgitate, and shit all over the northern shore. Half of the cove's trees have perished from exposure to the aggregate waste of nursery and outhouse. Muddy clumps of nests in the branches await the birds' return. Each year they reinforce them with twigs and herbaceous strands, clumps of roots, Styrofoam, and plastic. Birds weave knots not dissimilar to those sailors tie, lining the interiors of their nests with leaves and moss. The rookery, empty of its inhabitants, is ashen with excrement. Daryl turns the boat into Cane Lake, propelling them south.

When the white contingent arrived on motorboats and skiffs, Monique was at the front of the makeshift fleet, her maiden's head a Winged Victory, as if she were a sculpted prow. The Black runners couldn't shoot. Not at her. And understanding that it was Beau she had been calling upon, they were not surprised, but certainly put out, at the number he'd brought along, inebriated and armed, who were seeking justice, or thwarting it, depending on where you stood, land or lake. Leroy's men reached the shore without incident, muttering obscenities. The frogs croaked and the fires in the encampment burned, howling with wind. Monique led Beau up the steep incline, the ground slippery from the rain.

Disheartened over the sudden fall of their camp, most of Kyle's men retreated to the periphery of the fires. Their uneasy reluctance was reflected in the darting eyes of their intruders, the lack of purpose ubiquitous. Wary men on both sides recognized neighbors—men dealt with, if not daily, at least with familiarity, having worked for the same stingy contractors, traveled identical access roads, fished the bayous, and frequented the dilapidated country towns sporting music and fish festivals on their crooked shores. White men huddled together in a tight group. Talking sputtered, and a quiet discomfort settled in. Monique followed her father up the incline to the cabin.

Beau mounts the stairs slowly, eyeing the Black men lining the porch. Purposefully misguided, he does not entirely trust himself, or the circumstances that have brought him here: his son's death shrouded in mystery, his daughter's accusation unsupported. Murder is a phantom, and rumor follows him. The cabin's door is flung open to the elements. Beau quells the nausea in his stomach, flexes his shaking knees, and stops to gather conviction, but he hears the murmur of speculation. True and false wander together. A mob pushes speculation toward the outcome it craves. Rumor is wanton; something Beau knows well. He walks across the threshold. Inside, Noland shivers in expectation, but Jorge's snores fill the cabin.

When Beau sees the puckered skin and scabbed burns on Jorge's face, the captain's cap pulled over his eyes, this stranger with his legs arrogantly spread in sleep, he makes a silent oath. Even unconscious, Jorge simmers with virility;

Beau can smell it. No longer just imagining that this is the man who pulled the trigger and sent the bullet into his son's heart, he also understands, with a clanging finality, that this man did not order Michael's death. What slumbers before him is a henchman, at someone else's bidding. And so, in his moment of recognition, is Beau. Vengeance has its own momentum. Accepting the pact, Beau levels his rifle's muzzle and tips the cap off Jorge's head, then nudges the bridge between his eyes.

Jorge stirs as if swatting a fly, starts, and wakes.

"You have an appointment."

Jorge seeks balance and height all at once, his arms flail. The chair falls over, but he stands and registers Beau, his rifle, the shack littered with armed Black men and calls out for Noland.

Noland is fumbling outside on the porch, attempting to avoid further contact, insinuating himself next to Monique to impress the crowd with their alliance. His duplicitous gaze will not meet Jorge's as they march—Beau's gun in Jorge's back, Jorge's arms raised—out onto what will soon become a stage.

Beau pauses. "This him, baby?"

Monique can only nod yes, but her verdict spreads over the camp. The men gather beneath the cabin—white men's curiosity overcoming their uncertainty, uncertainty clamping the Black men's jaws. Jorge doesn't know fear yet; proud in his defeat, he spits a parting "Motherfucker" at Noland.

Beau shoves Jorge down the steps; bullying is inherent to complicity. Jorge sees the other cabins burning, and in the firelight, Leroy throws a gnarly rope, its hangman's noose a hollow abbreviation. It loops over the highest limb of a Bald Cypress at the camp's edge. Stricken, Jorge pleads up to Noland. "*Por qué*?" And still disbelieving, "*Ayúdame*."

Noland slinks behind Monique. She brushes the hair from her face and as if in prayer says, "Rot in hell."

Beau prods Jorge toward the tree. White men circle around them. But in the muddy clearing, Beau hands his gun to one of Leroy's men, and says to Jorge, "Hit me."

Jorge turns to him like a man possessed, his eyes wandering over an impassive flickering crowd. Beau lifts clenched fists and jabs his shoulder, prancing like a boxer. "Hit me."

In some dull hope that time will spare him, Jorge chooses to prolong his life. Beau does not raise his fists in defense but takes the cartilage crunching, blood-spewing blow full in the face and asks again.

Beau is not after salvation; sorrow and pain pursue him, and he's tired of running. Jorge hesitates, or perhaps, having glimpsed his future in the night stretching out past the fires, the rope swinging in gusts, he doesn't give a damn. Beau provokes him, slapping him as if he was a girl, and Jorge complies, punching him again and again. Fisticuffs sound like a nightstick on ripe fruit; sweat flies on impact. Each time Beau rises from the mud, the wind knocked from his lungs, blood dripping out of his mouth, he uses

Jorge to inflame his gluttony. Black men thinking: Get on with it man; white men always got to confuse the issue; you goin' to kill him, kill him. But the white men are too cold and groggy to stop Beau. Jorge, trapped by the circle of onlookers, resorts to an impressive, once-and-for-all punch just as Beau weaves out of range, ready to do damage.

Beau backs Jorge through the crowd toward the flames. His intention is to immolate them both, his son's maker and his son's killer, and quench the pain once and for all.

"That's enough." Leroy, disgusted, grabs Beau. "Do it right."

Beau, punch-drunk, falters.

Leroy's men, their motivation ambivalent from the beginning, could have stopped it at this point, taken Jorge into their charge and dropped him off at the jail, excluding the few who, masked and unrecognizable, had a hand in Percy and Skinner's slaughter. These men push forward, accusatory, intending to use Jorge's death to resolve all the killings and cover their own guilt. But it's Monique, seeing from her vantage point the rocking lights of Daryl's boat careen toward the island, who screams: "Kill him. Now!" She screams at Beau. "Kill him!"

Beau's anesthetized response, "This never happened," is taken as a warning, as if what's about to happen cannot be recorded. A tacit silence engulfs the crowd.

Jorge appeals to anyone. "*Ayúdame!*" His eyes search for Noland, but the space where Noland stood is empty.

It's a grim scene, with sullen men waiting around for it to

be over. Those from Leroy's group tie Jorge's hands behind his back and lift him up. His pulpy face is swollen with snot and blood, and he's begging for help. *"Creéme. No fui yo. Dios? Por favor. Dios mío."* Finally screaming, *"Dios!"*

They leave him under the noose, its rope angling from the limb like a pulley. Jorge bows his head in prayer.

Leroy calls to Beau. "You want the honors?"

Beau is slipping in and out of the present, a gaping hole, there and not there. This is his preamble to leaving; his mind shuts down; his body slumps; his thoughts, if any, are far away. His sense of time is so prolonged that flowers could take seed and fields grow from his back.

Monique yells to shake him from his stupor. "Kill him!"

It's Leroy who grabs the rope and pulls, stepping backward down the incline. Jorge's legs flail. Hemp constricts his shrieks to God. He's rising but he's not dying, the rope, caught under his chin, lifts him up, and the branch sags with his weight, a slow unyielding climb into darkness.

The scene fore and aft as Daryl enters the cove is far from pretty: Arevan stinks, and his puke is spewed all over the bow. The island is lit with fires, the night livid with light, awash with men, and Jorge's squirming from the rope like a kite flapping in the wind. From his vantage, Daryl can't see Monique, but he can hear her words whip through the air and vanish into the trees. "Kill him! Kill him"

The cove is so cluttered with skiffs that Daryl slams into a dozen on the way in. He doesn't slow down but plows his motorboat into the sandy shore, and it grinds to a halt. Arevan's thrown in place. Daryl unwraps the cleats and drags him like a roped steer, spitting and writhing, up the path to the circle. The mob is sullen, concentrating on the grim dance above them. They glance at Daryl tugging Arevan on the other end of his own rope, but that's a sideshow. Daryl is yelling that they don't know what they're doing when he hears a rifle's report. Jorge hangs from the rope, his neck stretched, his limbs limp, a hole in his chest. Beau pumps bullets into Jorge's torso, ripping flesh, eviscerating him.

Arevan pulls back. "Turn me over to them. They'll kill me for you. Turn me over to the state police, and I'll make sure it's Beau Duvet they charge with murder. Go ahead. Tell them they got it only half right. See how they justify the other half." Arevan looks up at Monique. She stares down at them from the porch, wrath shaking her frame. "And her: accessory to murder. Goaded him into it."

Sounds like a fucking lawyer, Daryl thinks, as if he'd consulted with his father—or the devil.

"And what did you do? Sold dope. I'll testify to that. You'll go to jail for a time, but Beau, maybe a life sentence, maybe a mental institution. How would you like that?"

It takes Daryl no time to drop the rope. Arevan will burn in hell: he'll see him there, when it's time.

He brushes past shivering men to Beau and touches his shoulder. Beau's in shock. Daryl takes him in his arms and holds him close. "Beau, I'm sorry."

Beau can't hear. He leans into Daryl's embrace. "Daryl, I'm so cold."

Daryl holds him tighter, rubbing his back. "Beau, please forgive me," is all he can say or think.

"Daryl, I can't make anything out."

They turn to water, their tears flowing. Men from the island cut down Jorge's body and carry it up to the cabin. Depleted by the spectacle, more men traipse down the slope to shore. Whites help Blacks untangle the lines, one holding a boat steady as the other climbs in. They're clearing the island, leaving it behind. Daryl takes one last look over his shoulder. The fires are burning themselves out, subsiding into embers. Monique remains on the stilted porch, a dark silhouette before their cabin door. He calls for her to come with them. She backs away, her body framed by light, wind tossing her hair. The wind is softer now, gusting like cotton. He calls to her again; supporting Beau, he can't let go of him. Kyle comes out of the cabin and puts his arm around Monique as if he owns her. It's her choice but not what Daryl wants; it bursts out of him like a horn. "Monique!"

And she comes flying down the stairs, throwing herself into his side. He almost stumbles as he catches her, grips both Monique and Beau as if they might blow away in the next gust and float like light from his arms.

Kyle throws a burning torch into the cabin. Inside, the shack glows; a window blows out. Daryl waits until Kyle descends its stairs, then turns toward the lake. They all leave together, a flotilla, Leroy's boat leading the way.

Someone else died, rather than any of them. Arevan is on one of the boats; he slunk his way into the crowd and blended into the pack. Daryl looks at the sky, blood red with dawn. Birds pirouette and skate above the horizon, plunge to the water, and jackknife back to the sky. Men, Black and white, ride the boats, each one euphoric to be going home. They've sacrificed a murderer, a hired hand. He came from no family that they knew, no home familiar to them, and had no allegiance to anyone they could identify. He was, in their lexicon, neither Black nor white, hated nor loved.

Daryl holds Beau; his arms can't keep him from shaking. He wonders what Beau sees: demons, he expects, or maybe nothing. Monique clings to Daryl and he hugs both close. He cannot leave them. They are what he's come back for.

# 30

# The Heronry

What happened? They all went home—they sat by the heater, ate breakfast, sighed with relief at their life. All of them loved a little harder, clung to their family members a little longer, and swore to give them sustenance. Guilt didn't tear them apart, poison their waters, or ruin their children. It brought them closer together. Now, when men meet each other on the street, they share a secret, and in that secret is a strength that feeds their resolve. Redeemed by a killer; that's what they say. They all bear the burden of complicity, and in knowing what they did, have something in common. Their eyes blank over at times, invert to thoughts not really forgotten. But they go on, sheltering each other from fear, and pushing the image of a man hanging from a tree back into the far reaches of their minds.

Monique and Daryl live together. They go to the festivals, dance away their mourning, and celebrate the fact they're living by swooping around the dance floor like birds. In joy, and finally, humility, something Daryl has learned: there's relief but no release. He visits Michael's grave and prays, to whom he's not sure, but he prays. And he walks into his mother's shining cane fields, her plants high, the sun full, and kneels in the sandy soil where he prays again: for the rains to come, for the harvest to be full, for the new shoots to grow. He plays Chopin's sonatas and nocturnes, compositions his mother taught him; he can hear her humming the chords, the notes slipping from her breath as she played. Sometimes at night, he cries in Monique's arms. She bears the loss better than anyone. Daryl is guilty, but Monique did what she had to do for love, for him. They're not married yet, but they will be as soon as their first child is born. Monique doesn't want to wear a wedding dress until she has a waist again. They plan for her to carry their baby down the aisle in her arms. The hall will be packed, and in their union, their celebration, they'll help each other to endure. Daryl's hung the photograph of his mother holding him in her arms in the baby's room; she's waiting there for her grandchild. His father? Let him rot in the fortress of his own making and go to hell.

Arevan has returned to his former life as Jacques Navera; he no longer ferries men to and from the rigs; he captains his shrimp boat. One of the debts he owed has been paid in full; the other won't be paid in this lifetime. Beau wafts away on occasion, but he always comes back. He sits on the back porch in Michael's chair and watches dark birds circle a pale white sun. Mae stays at Beau's for good now. Monique and Daryl spend time with them, coaxing Beau out to the clubs, where he plays music better than before. Sorrow has done that for him. Noland disappeared, and no one seems to have noticed. Kyle's forming a union; he runs the mill. And Daryl? Daryl lays bricks for a living; he has his own crew, familiar faces from Cane Island. They build houses, fortifications against the elements, the dark night, the enigmatic swamp. One brick next to and then on top of another, his trowel slapping mortar, and before Daryl knows it, a home. He looks up when the sun's high and listens for the cry of birds.

Birds fly to survive. They flock in a swirling mass, a fortress against predators, or in restless migration to food supplies; labor to feed their young or spread wings to dance in courtship. Men fly to escape, to leave for someplace else, to find something other than what they have. They're searching for God. That's what men long for when they watch birds soar, a state of grace. When an alligator or a raccoon steals a nestling, birds screech in pain and warning, lift talons and spread wings to leap in grief. And when mates are injured or die, they do not abandon them, but fly overhead to call out in sorrow, or roost to guard their remains. And when hordes of birds spiral from sky to earth at sunset, it's in joy. Chests buoyed by air, backs warmed by sun, wings spread in prayer. Mourning those who fall in flight, they whirl like locusts to rise and plummet, a din for those they've lost, their brethren in sustenance and propagation. Love is sustenance. Those who love are blessed with grace.

Ardea, smothered in flames, lay in ruins. The first heron rose from its ashes, flapped and beat embers with gray-blue wings, its call the call of lamentation. Cane Island's northern tip, the station of the birds, from where men could smell the stench and sweetness of life, will rise from the swamp again, a riotous jungle of birds, cane, and sky. The birds, our messengers to and from the gods, will remind us of its unrelenting cycle.

I thank my guides in this endeavor: Anney Bonney, Tina Girouard, Dickie Landry, and Garland Fredrick. My core: Gary Indiana, Patrick McGrath and Lynne Tillman. More friends who acted as readers, providers of sanctuary, or advisers: Marti Blumenthal, Rosemary Carroll, Emery Clark, Michael Coffey, Giuliana Bruno and Andrew Fierberg, Coleen Fitzgibbon, David Deutsch and Shawn Gannon, Nicole Klagsbrun, Ira Silverberg, Klaus Kertess and Billy Sullivan, Joan Sussler, Virginia Taylor, and Michael Zwack. My former, intrepid agent, Emma Sweeney, and my literary agent, the brilliant author Madison Smartt Bell; and my publisher, T Thilleman and Spuyten Duyvil for their courage.

No book comes into existence without the experiences and accumulated knowledge of others. Tina Girouard and Dickie Landry welcomed me to their homeland and told me their stories. The Atchafalaya swamp and its environs were inspiration. The research books follow: *The Arabian Nights*; *The Birds* by Aristophanes—from the series Encyclopedia Britannica, Great Books, translated by Benjamin Bickley Rogers, and *Four Plays by Aristophanes*, translated by William Arrowsmith; The New Oxford Annotated Bible; *White Ibis* by Keith L. Bildstein; *Rites and Symbols of Initiation* by Mircea Eliade; Ovid's *Metamorphoses*, translated by Charles

Boer; *The Homeric Poems*, the Charles Boer translation; *The Dream and the Underworld*, by James Hillman; The Eranos Lectures 2 and 8 —*The Thought of the Heart* and *On Paranoia* —by James Hillman; *Oedipus Variations* by Karl Kerenyi and James Hillman; *Pan and the Nightmare* by William Heinrich Roscher and James Hillman; *Essays on a Science of Mythology* by C.J. Jung and C. Kerenyi; *Hermes Guide of Souls* and *Eleusis* by Karl Kerenyi; *Sacrifice* by Henry Hubert and Marcel Mauss; *The Lives of Birds* by Lester L. Short; *On Dreams and Death* by Maria-Louise von Franz, and *Drugs, Addiction, and Initiation: The Modern Search for Ritual* by Luigi Zoja.

Of course, ultimately, the characters demand their own accounting.

Betsy Sussler attended Newcomb, the women's college of Tulane University in New Orleans and graduated from the San Francisco Art Institute with a BFA in 1974. She cofounded BOMB Magazine in 1981 to publish conversations between artists and writers that reflected the way they spoke about the work among themselves and has been its Editor in Chief ever since. Sussler has edited five anthologies: *BOMB Interviews*, City Lights (1991); *BOMB: Speak Art!* (1997), *Speak Fiction and Poetry!* (1998) and *Speak Theater and Film!* (1999), published by Gordon and Breach; and *The Author Interviews* (2014) published by Soho Press. This is her first novel, *Station of the Birds*, written in the late 90s. She lives and works in Brooklyn, New York with her two felines, Calliope and Woody Ray.

www.ingramcontent.com/pod-product-compliance
Lightning Source LLC
Chambersburg PA
CBHW010610310726
48969CB00010B/2641